Love Hurts

TARA CONRAD

HIS ONE HER ONLY PUBLISHING

Contents

To all those whose light continues to shine in the darkness.

Note to Readers

A Note to My Readers,

This book contains dark and, at times, violent themes. Please don't hesitate to put your mental health first and read with caution. For a full list of content please visit my website.

Check Content Warnings Here

Anthony

SEPTEMBER 10, 2001

Excitement courses through me. I feel like a child creeping down the steps on Christmas morning, waiting to see the gifts Santa left under the tree. I know I'm not a child, and what's about to happen—it's the culmination of years of hard work, but the magic is still the same.

Kameron and I exit the subway on West Fourth and walk the last few blocks to Macdougal Street, where we'll sign the lease for my new restaurant. Opening an Italian restaurant has been my dream since I was a little boy. Many of my fondest childhood memories are of being in Nonna's kitchen. She'd stand me on a chair next to her so I could reach the counter. I was happiest with my hands in a dough or figuring out what ingredients our sauce needed.

She instilled in me a love for food. Not the pre-packed stuff, but the kind you pick from the earth and mix together to make a nourishing and delicious meal. Nonna taught me that cooking and serving food is more than a chore. It's a delight and something I learned to take great pride and satisfaction in.

My dream of becoming a chef began all those years ago. Studying, training, saving, and waiting for the right location to become available. Finally, everything's lined up, and my dream's about to come true.

"Have I told you how proud I am of you, Sir?" Kam asks as he squeezes my hand gently.

"You have, *amore mio*." I smile lovingly at the man by my side.

Kameron and I met while I was still in culinary school. I was working as a sous chef at *Flavour*, an upscale restaurant in midtown when he came in one night with a small group of people. It was a stroke of luck or perhaps fate that he and I met. Emmanuel, the Owner and Executive Chef, had a family emergency and reached out at the last minute for my help.

"I'm at the hospital. Beth went into labor with the twins," Chef Emmanuel says when I answer the phone. "She's early. It wasn't supposed to happen like this."

The chef and his wife had been trying to conceive for years. After several rounds of IVF, she finally got pregnant. To say he's been a nervous father-to-be is an understatement.

Emmanuel took a chance on me when I graduated high school and hired me. Arguably, I've learned more in his kitchen than in my two years of culinary school. "What do you need me to do?"

"The FDNY has a reservation tonight. There's a young hotshot in the department. What's his name?" Papers rustle in the background. "Here it is. Kameron Harlow. He's being promoted to Captain of the Midtown Firehouse. It's a big deal because he's only thirty-two and the youngest Captain in the FDNY."

"What do I need to know?" I ask confidently.

Chef takes a few minutes to give me the instructions for the event, which include a personal visit from me to their table to thank them all for their service to the city.

"Fuck, Anthony. I can't put this on you." His voice is strained. "Running the restaurant is my responsibility. I shouldn't be passing this on to—."

"Emmanuel," I say his name loudly, hoping to stop him. "Your wife is in labor. That's exactly where your attention should be." I lower my voice, "Don't worry about the restaurant. I can handle it."

"*Are you sure?*" he asks.

"*I'm positive.*"

I'll never forget the first time Kameron's eyes met mine. I was standing beside their table holding a bottle of Bollinger La Grand Année when he looked up, and I saw the most beautiful amber eyes. I stood there with my mouth hanging open. It felt like hours, but in reality, it was probably only seconds that I stood there before I found my words.

"On behalf of Flavour, we'd like to extend our sincerest gratitude to the Midtown Firehouse for their service to our city." I turn to face the guest of honor. "I'd also like to personally congratulate Captain Harlow on his recent promotion."

While the men and women at the table applaud, I pop the cork on the bottle of champagne and pour the new Captain's glass first.

"Thank you, Chef," he says, gracing me with a dazzling smile.

"It's my pleasure." His eyes follow me as I make my way around the table, pouring everyone's drinks. "If I can be of any further service, please let me know." With a final glance at the sexy firefighter, I return to the kitchen.

Even though it's a busy night, I struggle to stay focused. My mind keeps returning to the man being celebrated in the dining room.

I'm putting the finishing touches on a dessert plate when one of the servers pops her head into the pastry room. "Hey, Chef," she calls.

"What's up?"

"That hot firefighter is asking to speak to you."

My hand freezes mid-movement. Regaining my composure, I say, "Tell him I'll be out in a minute, please."

"Will do." She starts to go back out into the restaurant but stops. With her hand on the doorway, she turns around. "Do you think you can manage to slip him my number?" I raise my eyebrows disapprovingly. She holds her hands up in surrender and giggles. "Can't blame a girl for trying."

I wash my hands and hurry to the restaurant floor, but he's no longer at the table. I hope he hasn't left already. Looking around, I spot him near the hostess station, leaning against the wall. His arms are crossed over his well-defined chest, making his white button-down dress shirt pull tight around his shoulders.

When he sees me coming, he pushes off the wall. "I'm sorry for taking you away from your job," he says as I get closer.

"It's not a problem. What can I do for you?"

"I just wanted to say—" He stops and bites his bottom lip.

"Was everything to your liking?" I ask, worrying our service didn't live up to his expectations.

"Yes." He laughs softly. "It's nothing like that. I was wondering if you'd like..." He blows out a breath as he runs his fingers through his wavy black hair. "This was a bad idea. Thanks again for every-thing." Kameron turns to walk away, but I reach out and touch his arm, stopping him.

"Wait." My voice is low. "I'd like to talk to you more, but we don't close for another hour."

"I'll come back," he says quickly.

His promise echoes in my mind for the rest of the evening. Thankfully, there's only one table left—the night's almost over. The back and front of the house get cleaned in record time. After the last employee leaves, I make my way to the front.

I glance outside and am surprised to see Kameron standing by the light post. Part of me was uncertain whether he'd show up or not. My hands tremble as I switch off the lights and step outside. I lock the door before walking over to him. "Hi."

"Hi," he says, and a smile spreads across his face. He kicks at a small pebble on the sidewalk. "Would you like to grab some drinks?"

A bar or club with loud music and people crammed shoulder to shoulder is not my scene. I can't let this opportunity, this man, slip through my fingers, though. So, I take a risk and do something I've never done before. "How about we go back to my place?"

We went home together that night and have been together ever since.

A few months later, I introduced Kameron to the BDSM life-style. Although it was something new to him, it came naturally.

His job in the FDNY is high-stress and demanding. It often requires split-second, life-altering decisions. Kam's submission allows him to relax. To let someone else take the responsibility for him and make the decisions.

"Mr. Genovese," Charlie, the realtor, says, shaking my hand vigorously. "It's a pleasure to see you again." He turns to Kam. "You as well, Chief Harlow. Congratulations on your recent promotion."

Kam's still with the FDNY and was recently promoted to Chief at the Midtown Firehouse. "Thank you," he responds.

"Let's get down to business." Charlie motions toward what's left of the bar from the previous business. "Let's get these papers signed."

The windows have been covered with heavy-duty butcher paper, blocking any light from outside. That, combined with the dim lighting inside, makes it challenging to read through the document in a timely fashion. Or perhaps it's my anxiousness to get this part over with so we can move forward with the rest of my plans.

When we leave here, we're going to have a romantic dinner at *Flavour*. Then, we're going to stop by the apartment to grab the bags I packed and head to the airport for a late night flight to Bermuda. Tomorrow is our tenth anniversary. It's also when I plan to ask Kameron to wear my collar.

In my pocket is a black leather collar I can't wait to fasten around his neck. Unlike most submissive collars, it won't be locked. Because of his job, it needs to be easily removable. The thought of my sexy firefighter submissive wearing a symbol of my possession makes my dick hard. I'm grateful for the bar in front of me that hides my erection. I have to force my thoughts back to the task at hand —signing my lease.

I'm skimming the last page when Kam's cell rings. "It's the station. I have to take this." He excuses himself while I sign each notated line.

"Congratulations," Charlie says and hands me the keys. "I can't wait to see what you do with the place."

I walk him to the door just as Kam ends his call. "I'll catch a train and be there in about twenty minutes."

My heart sinks. It's not uncommon for Kameron to get called into work on his day off. It's part of the job. In the beginning, it wasn't easy. I worked long hours and late nights, and Kam often got called in at the last minute. It put a lot of stress on us. But we were committed to making our relationship work. Now, it's just par for the course. But tonight, I feel a pang of disappointment. "You have to go in?"

"There's a multi-station emergency," Kam explains as he slides his cell into his pocket.

"Is it something Bailey can handle?" I ask.

"He's out of town." I knew I was taking a chance buying plane tickets for just after midnight when Kam would be on call this evening. "What's wrong?" he asks.

"I planned a romantic evening for us." I don't tell him about the trip. If he's going to a call, he doesn't need to be worried about it. I bought insurance on the trip just in case. "I can reschedule."

"I'll be home as soon as I can. Then we have the rest of the week together."

"That sounds great," I say, trying to mask my disappointment. "Text me when you get there."

"I will." Kam turns to walk away, but I catch his arm and pull him back to me, intending to give him a quick kiss goodbye.

As if my hand has a mind of its own, it grabs him by the back of his neck pulling him to me. Our kiss quickly becomes heated. Kam's erection presses against my stomach. I pull away, leaving both of us breathless. "When your shift is over, you're turning that damn cellphone off so we can have a proper celebration."

"That can be arranged," he says with a grin. "I love you."

"I love you more." I step outside and watch as he walks down the street. Once he's out of sight, I go back inside.

I'm not in a hurry to go home alone. Instead, I peel the paper off the windows, letting the bright lights from the outside stream into the space. Already, it feels more alive. Tomorrow morning, the contractors will arrive to start the renovations. In just a few weeks, this space will go through a complete transformation and become *Italiano Desiderio*.

A crack of thunder reminds me we're expecting some heavy storms. I give Chef Emmanuel a quick call to let him know I have to cancel our reservations and then hurry home before the worst of the storms hit.

Kameron

SEPTEMBER 11, 2001

Tony tried to hide his disappointment from me, but I could still see it. It's been that way since the night we met. Tony wears his heart on his sleeve, and his face is the canvas that reveals every emotion.

Leaving him standing there alone gutted me, but it's part of the job. I'd hoped to be home already, but we had call after call last night. When it finally quieted down, it was closing in on four a.m., and I was exhausted. Instead of trying to stumble home half asleep, I decided to crash at the station and go home today.

The sun is just peeking above the horizon. So far, it's been quiet. I promised the guys a nice breakfast, but right now, they're still asleep. I take advantage of the quiet and go for a run. The early hour means I avoid the congestion on the streets that's certain to come later.

I gaze up at the crystal-clear azure blue sky, marveling at its striking beauty. The storms from yesterday have moved out, blanketing the city in a serene tranquility.

I almost hate to go back inside. Buying myself a few extra minutes, I text Emmanuel.

Me: Is it possible to get a reservation for two for tonight?

Chef E: For you, anything. What time?

Me: Can we make it about 8?

Chef E: Done. See you both tonight.

Now, to let Tony know.

Me: I made reservations for us tonight at *Flavour* so we can have a proper celebration.

It might be a bit of topping from the bottom, but I don't think he'll mind.

My World: I have a little something planned for tonight, too. Dinner will be the perfect appetizer.

Me: That sounds intriguing.

My World: When should I expect you home?

Me: I promised the guys a hot breakfast. I'll be home shortly after.

My World: Sounds good. Text me when you're on your way. I love you.

Me: Will do. I love you, too.

When I get inside, the guys are up and around. I was hoping for a quick shower, but that'll have to wait until I get home.

"We thought you ditched us here," Marcus says, elbowing me jokingly.

"And have all of you starve? Not a chance. I don't want my vacation interrupted." Everyone laughs.

I'm thankful they put the coffee on while I was out because I need a caffeine fix. Maybe I'm getting too old for this? Who am I kidding? Firefighting is my life. I couldn't see myself being happy doing anything else.

I pull the eggs and bacon out of the fridge and start cooking. Never knowing when we'll get called out ensures we don't waste time getting things done here. Twenty minutes later, the food is done, and we're sitting down to eat when the alarm sounds.

It's just after 8:46 when a call comes in that a plane has crashed into the North Tower of the World Trade Center. I grab a slice of bacon and hurry to my truck, where the chauffeur is already waiting behind the wheel.

While we're en route, my phone rings. I don't check the caller ID before answering.

"FDNY. Harlow speaking."

"Kam, it's me," Tony stammers, his voice trembling. "Are you on your way to the tower?"

"Yeah. We got a call about a plane hitting it. Must've been an inexperienced pilot or engine trouble."

"I have the news on. People are saying it was a commercial jet."

"A jet?" I ask in disbelief. My driver glances at me curiously before returning his focus to the road ahead. "Are you sure?"

"It was impossible not to hear. It echoed through the house." His voice quivers. "It's bad, Kam. There's no way anyone survived."

"We're pulling up now. I have to go." I don't wait for the car to come to a complete stop before I jump out.

"Please be careful, Kam."

"Will do." I disconnect the call and look up, horrified by what I see. There's a massive hole in the tower with flames and black smoke billowing out. I hurry to the makeshift command post across the street to get my orders.

The FDNY chief is already on the scene. "Harlow, I want you in the North Tower helping with the evacuations."

"Yes, sir," I respond and then sprint across the eight-lane highway.

9:03 AM

The roar of the jet engine flying low—too low, is deafening. The ground below my feet shakes from the force. A fireball erupts from the building. I shield my face from the almost unbearable heat and debris. Blinking, I force myself to look up. The plane is gone. It disappeared into the side of the South Tower.

My ears ring, but it doesn't drown out the sound of terrified screams around me. Steel pieces from the building or the decimated jet rain down. Seconds later, a person, I can't tell a man or woman, runs outside. Her body's on fire. She drops to the ground, rolling around to extinguish the flames.

If there was any doubt that the first plane was an accident, it's gone now. This was a deliberate attack.

Anthony

I HAVE AN ALMOST DIRECT VIEW OF THE BURNING tower from our Tribeca home. I watch the plumes of smoke rising from the tower in disbelief. In the background, the news anchors speculate about what may or may not have happened. I'm glued to the scene, plagued with a sense of uneasiness.

I'm holding my cellphone when it rings. "Hello?"

"Did you see the news?" Star asks frantically.

"I'm watching it out my window."

"Is Kameron with you?"

"No. He's down there."

"Do you know what happened?"

"Other than the speculation from reporters and what I'm seeing outside, I have no idea."

"When Kam lets you—"

My hand slips from my ear when a second plane flying at my eye level comes into view. "Oh my God." The words come out in a whisper as the jet slams into the South Tower and explodes. The force of the impact shakes my building.

"What was that?" Star screams. "Tony." I don't answer. I can't speak. "Anthony. Are you there? What's going on?"

My hand shakes as I bring the phone back to my ear. "It was another plane," I manage to say, struggling to articulate the gravity of the situation. "Something terrible is going on."

Kameron

9:05AM

Glass shatters. Footsteps pound on the pavement. Sirens fill the air.

The scene looks like something from a horror movie. As far as the eye can see, everything is blanketed in a thick covering of ash and debris. Fire blazes from the top floors of the two towers. Thick smoke fills the air, making it difficult to breathe. I grab the emergency uniform and SCBA gear from the back of my truck and suit up.

Shattered windows line the structures. People lean out frantically, waving anything at their disposal in an attempt to signal rescuers to their location.

Marcus sidles up next to me. "What's the plan, Chief?"

"Get your—" My answer is cut short when two figures, hands clasped together, jump from an upper floor of the tower. "My God," I whisper.

"We can't reach them." Marcus's voice sounds faraway. "How do we get them out?"

"We have to go in. There's no other way."

After I give Marcus the orders for his team, I go against the flow through the crowds of people running out of the buildings.

Some are hysterical. Their expressions reflect pure terror as they push their way to safety. Others wander, their eyes wide and faces covered in soot. They're in shock. As much as I want to stop and help them, I can't. These people are out—they're safe. Inside those towers are countless others—they're my target.

Darkness envelopes the space, illuminated only by the beams of flashlights from myself and the other emergency responders. Navigating through the shadows, I head towards the stairwell and climb the steps two at a time. Along the way, I encounter people hurrying down, trying to get to the exit.

"I can't see where to go." A woman cries. "Someone help me, please."

"I'm right here." Grabbing her arm, I put her hand against the wall to help her get oriented. "Keep your hand on the wall," I yell so she can hear me over the commotion. "Don't stop until you're outside."

I wait a second to ensure she follows my command before I continue my trek up.

9:40AM

"Harlow." Miller's staticky voice comes through my walkie. "Do you read me?"

"I can barely hear you," I respond to my boss.

"The Pentagon was hit a few minutes ago. Reports are there's one more hijacked plane unaccounted for."

I stop momentarily to catch my breath. "We're under attack?"

"Unofficially, yes."

9:59AM

Not knowing for sure what's going on outside, I try to concentrate on clearing each floor, pointing the inhabitants toward the stairwell and eventual safety. "Go toward the lights," I yell, knowing those are my brothers and sisters below. "Don't stop moving."

While I climb to the next floor, I listen to the radio calls. Another battalion chief in the South Tower was able to fix a broken service elevator. He and his crew are at the top, evacuating the occupants.

"We have people jumping out here." A call comes across the radio. "How the hell bad is it up there?"

Metal twists and groans. The sound reverberates through the massive structure as if it's crying out in agony. The building shudders with such intensity that I need to cling to the handrail for dear life. Terrified screams join the chaos. Time stretches, creating an illusion that the unsettling tremors persist for an eternity, though in truth, only mere seconds have elapsed.

"What the hell is going on out there?" I yell into my walkie.

The staticky reply comes through. "The South Tower fucking collapsed."

There's no way I heard him correctly. "Can you repeat that?"

"The South Tower is gone."

Collapsed?

Gone?

I can't comprehend what I'm being told. My heart echoes loudly in my chest, a relentless percussion matching the uncertain fate that hangs in the air.

"Get the fuck out of there, Harlow."

I can't leave when there are more people in here. Ignoring the order, I continue on.

"Is anyone there?" A woman's voice calls from the darkness.

I point my flashlight in the direction of the sound and find a visibly pregnant woman huddled in the corner. "I'm right here," I say as I defy every rule ingrained in me and pull off my SCBA apparatus. The air hangs heavy with smoke and debris, triggering immediate coughing on my part. "Put this on. Just breathe normal," I instruct and strap the tank to her back. "It might be heavy." I choke. "But it'll give you clean air until we get you out. Ready to go?" With a nod, she signals her readiness, and I assist her to her feet amidst the challenging conditions.

Guided by the faint glow of my flashlight, we start down the steps. We make it down ten floors before meeting up with a small group accompanied by several other first responders. Their familiar silhouettes materialize in the dim illumination.

"Did you clear the floor?" I yell.

"Yes," an NYPD officer replies.

"Take her." I hand the woman over. "Make sure she gets out. I'm going back up."

10:15AM

Despite the groans emanating from the structure, I persist in my search. My body screams, but I ignore it. I have one purpose, evacuating as many individuals as I can to ensure their safety. The atmosphere is dense, the air carrying a palpable weight that makes breathing increasingly challenging. Unsuccessful in finding anyone on the current floor, I try to go up, but my path is completely blocked by a large steel beam. I'm forced to turn around. On each floor, I test the doors and call out into the darkness, conducting a quick sweep for anyone we might have missed.

10:26AM

I make my way down to the next level. The structural groans reverberate with heightened intensity, creating an ominous soundtrack. I come to a door, but it's jammed. Frustration mounts with each kick and shove, the unyielding door adding an extra layer of difficulty and exacerbating the challenge of breathing.

Gasping for clean air, my lungs cry out in desperation as I slump against the wall. A grim awareness settles over me. I fumble around in my pocket, looking for my cell, desperately hoping for a stroke of mercy that would allow me to make a call.

I try Tony's number over and over and am met with a busy signal each time. I'm ready to give up when it finally rings through.

"Kam, is that you?"

"Yes, Sir." I cough into my arm. "It's me."

"Where are you?"

"I'm in the North Tower." I manage through the smokey air.

"How far up are you?"

"Stairwell B Thirtieth Floor."

"The South Tower collapsed," Tony says through his tears. "You have to get out. Now."

"I don't have my oxygen." My voice is raspy. "I'm not going to make it out."

"Don't say that. I'll call 911 and tell them—"

"Stop." I choke. "I need you to listen to me." I hear the soft sound of his tears. "Do you remember the night we first met?"

"How could I forget?"

"I was so scared when I asked that waitress to get you. I had no clue about your preferences, but I couldn't leave without finding out. It would've haunted me for the rest of my life."

"Kam, please keep trying."

I ignore his pleas and continue, "The way you held me in your protective embrace. I've never felt so cherished. I fell in love that night, and each day for the past ten years, I've only grown to love you more."

"I planned a trip for us. To celebrate."

"Where are we going?"

"Bermuda," Tony says through his tears. "I had a collar made for you. Will you accept it, *amore mio*?"

"I'd love nothing more." Tears slide down my face as I struggle to take each breath. "I'm yours, Sir. I've always have been."

"Then, come home to me. Let me show you how much I love you."

An unsettling groan emanates from the tower, a sound that echoes with the weight of its own existence, sending shivers through the air.

"I'm not going to make it out, Anthony." I cover my head from the falling debris.

An immediate influx of air surrounds me, then another, each conveying an unsettling narrative. The sound bears an eerie resemblance to that ominous moment when the first tower collapsed.

"Never forget how much I love you."

The foreboding sensation intensifies as I am consumed by a visceral awareness of the imminent disaster, a palpable recognition that the tower is collapsing. The phone slips from my grasp.

"Kameron," Anthony screams desperately.

At that moment, an unexpected calmness blankets me. A still, serene acceptance permeates my soul. There's no fear, even as the thunderous crash of eighty floors collapses around me. Enveloped in tranquility, I close my eyes. In that darkness, I see Tony's loving gaze, a comforting sight as I accept the end has come.

Anthony

Hours may have passed, or maybe just moments. Time has become meaningless as I stare vacantly at the space where the Twin Towers stood.

"Tony," Star's voice carries a gentle, soft tone. "Owen and I are here," she reassures, her hand reaching out to touch my arm. "Why don't you come sit down? I'll make some tea." Despite her gentle tug on my arm, I find myself resisting her suggestion.

"Go put some water on," Owen says. "I'll stay with him." He moves closer to me. "They're finding people. We'll hear from him."

"No, we won't," I say absently.

"You have to stay positive." Owen encourages.

"He was on the thirtieth floor. I was on the phone with him when it collapsed." Silent tears make their way down my cheeks. "Kam told me he loves me. I saw it start before I heard it." The sound. I'll never forget the horrible sound. The desperate anguish of the metal, followed by the thunderous roar of the concrete, consuming not just the structure but everything in its way—including Kameron. "Then it was silent, and the line went dead." I shift my focus to Owen. "I can feel it in here. He's gone."

Something shatters inside me, and I fall to my knees, curling in on myself. Owen's arms wrap around me, offering refuge as I lose myself in the dark abyss of grief.

My mind and body are numb as I allow Owen to lead me to the sofa. Outside, the blue sky that was pristine sapphire is now shadowed by an ominous ashen canopy. I struggle to wrap my head around the reality of what I've just witnessed. The two iconic towers that are an integral part of this city have crumbled into nothing more than a pile of smoldering rubble.

Every channel on television has ceased its regular broadcast. Newscasters openly shed tears as they try to cover this monstrous yet historical event. Our country and the world are trying to comprehend what we've witnessed today. Not only did New York City come under attack, but a third plane flew into the Pentagon, killing countless more people.

An ordinary group of people, now hailed as heroes, were on a fourth hijacked plane. As they got phone calls out to family members, they learned their destination was most likely the White House. These passengers made the brave choice to storm the cockpit and take the plane down in a field in Pennsylvania. Their lives weren't spared, but countless others were.

I refuse to accept this is the end. Denial kicks in, and I jump up. "I need to go down there."

"I don't think that's possible," Star says gently.

"Kam's alone," I insist. "I need to be there for him."

"Tony," she says as tears cascade down her cheeks. "It's not safe."

"I don't care. I'm going." I brush past her, but Owen intervenes, blocking my path. "Move out of my way," I persist, frustration evident in my tone.

"That's not happening," he insists, crossing his arms.

"You can either stay here or come with me to find him: your choice, but either way, I'm going."

Owen and I are locked in a battle of wills, but I refuse to back down. When Owen's arms drop to his sides, I know I've won. "Stay here," Owen says to Star.

"You can't go down there." Star's nearly frantic.

"I'll take him as close as possible."

"Owen, please," Star pleads. "What if there's more attacks?"

"If we allow fear to dictate our lives, then we let whoever fucking did this win." Anger, not directed at Star, is evident in his tone. "And that can't happen," he softens his voice. "All flights have been grounded. We're as safe as we can be." He looks at me. "It's something he needs to do."

"It's a good thing we brought these," Owen says, pointing to the white rags we're holding over our faces.

Outside resembles scenes from a dystopian movie. A thick blanket of ash cloaks the entirety of lower Manhattan. Papers from the offices within the towers now scatter the streets like apocalyptic confetti. The air is dense with smoke, and sirens wail relentlessly in every direction. However, in a stark departure from the ordinary, the streets are devoid of traffic. Only emergency responders navigate the debris-riddled streets until they're forced to abandon their vehicles to proceed on foot toward the site.

As we draw nearer, the surreal nature of the situation intensifies. It's midday on a Tuesday, and we're walking down the middle of the six-lane West Side Highway. Numerous people, their faces masked in ash, wander aimlessly with vacant stares, undoubtedly mirroring my own.

Approaching the site, the air is pierced by the unsettling chirping of hundreds of PASS devices, a haunting reminder of firefighters in distress. One of those belongs to Kameron. The thought of him trapped somewhere in the rubble, injured and alone, wondering if rescue will come, is agonizing.

"I'm sorry. You can't go any further." An officer stops the small group we've caught up with before turning his back on us to attend to something else.

"I need to get through," I protest and try to push my way through.

He grabs my arm to stop me. "Sir. I can't let you—"

Instantly, I recognize him. "Graham, I have to find Kameron."

"Tony," he says, his voice strained. "I can't let you through."

"He was in the North Tower when it collapsed. Please," I beg, grabbing his hand. "I have to find him."

"Our rescue teams are in there," he tries to assure me. "We'll get them all out."

"I can help," I insist and once again try to push my way past, but Graham puts his hands on my chest, stopping me.

"It's too dangerous." I ignore his directives and continue to struggle. "Anthony," Graham yells my name. "You'll be more of a liability if you go in there. If Kameron survived, he's going to need you in one piece, not injured from being in the middle of that." He stabs his finger in the direction of the fire that burns in the remnants of buildings. "For now, the best thing you can do for Kameron and everyone else is to give them space to do their jobs." He softens his voice and his bottom lip quivers. "My partner was in there, too. I know how much it goddamn hurts to not be over there."

"I can't go home and sit around waiting for a call that he's dead." Pain sears my chest. "I have to do something."

"This is going to be a massive effort," Owen interjects. "These men and women are going to need help to sustain them. Let's go back to your place and use our resources to make that happen. Okay?"

My eyes travel between Owen and Graham, then fixate on the area where the majestic buildings once graced the city's skyline. The gravity of the situation leaves me breathless. They're gone. Reduced to a massive pile of debris—a final resting place for many souls.

Later that evening, as the sun begins to set on what is easily the worst day in the lives of all of us, we watch the continuing news coverage. Lawmakers in Washington D.C. gather on the steps of the Capital Building to address the nation, promising solidarity as we seek justice for the evil committed against us.

In a poignant moment that will not soon be forgotten, the men and women set aside their political affiliations and previous disagreements. Their collective focus shifts to the shared identity that binds us as Americans, uniting their voices in the rendition of "God Bless America."

Anthony

Owen and Star haven't left my house since they arrived Tuesday. Part of me wishes they'd go so I could be alone with my thoughts and sorrow, while the other part is thankful for their constant presence. With every minute that passes, the gaping hole in my heart grows. I'm afraid it will swallow me whole.

When we left the pile the other day, Owen and I devised a plan to try to meet some of the rescuers' needs. I knew I'd need Emmanuel to help make my idea successful.

I tried for hours to get him on the phone, but with the lines down, it was impossible. So, I took a chance and walked to the restaurant. I found him alone, his head in his hands as the television at the bar broadcasted the continued narrative. Together, we made a plan and started putting it in motion. Today, we begin implementing it.

The sky is still dark when Owen, Star, and I arrive at the restaurant. Emmanuel's already there, along with his two adult sons.

"Have you heard anything?" he asks when I walk into the kitchen.

My heart sinks knowing other than a handful of firefighters

who were rescued just hours after the collapse, no one else has been found. "No."

"Don't give up," he encourages me.

I offer a faint smile but remain silent, fearing that the fragile threads holding me together will unravel if I speak.

"Where can we help?" Star asks, taking the attention off of me.

"How are you at cooking eggs?" Dylan, Emmanuel's oldest son, asks.

"I think I can manage those."

Star joins him, making dozens of scrambled eggs. Owen and I fry bacon and sausage while Emmanuel and his younger son, Micah, make grits and toast. When we have enough for a small army, we load up the van and head toward lower Manhattan.

I'm not sure how, but the sights around us appear worse today than they did immediately following the disaster. The ash is settling and is thicker than it was. Cars sit abandoned and likely unusable. Every few blocks, we see a twisted metal beam or the remains of office furniture.

What strikes me the most are the photocopied pictures of people—thousands of loved ones frozen in time, that haven't been accounted for. They're hanging from every available surface. A silent plea for a miracle.

The twenty-four-hour mark signaled a grim reality that shifted the mission from rescue to recovery. Because the pile is so unstable, old-fashioned bucket brigades are being utilized to painstakingly sift through the debris for any remains. The work is tedious and dangerous as workers must deal with jagged pieces of metal and scorching fires that continue to burn. In a morbid request, rescue workers have been instructed to write their names and contact information on their arms in case they, too, become victims of this heinous tragedy.

But I, like countless others, have chosen not to give in to despair. The idea of a future without Kameron by my side is unfathomable. Instead, I cling to the hope that despite all odds,

Kameron will be found, and we'll emerge from this darkness together.

Our SUV rolls to a stop when we reach a barricade.

An office approaches, and Emmanuel rolls down his window. "I'm sorry. Only emergency vehicles can pass," the officer says.

"We made arrangements with Commissioner to deliver food," Emmanuel explains.

"One minute." He walks away from our car to talk to another officer. They both look back at us before the first officer returns. "There's a spot two blocks down on the right for you to set up."

"That's perfect. Thank you," Emmanuel says.

As we inch through the final few blocks, we find tired rescue workers leaning against their vehicles, seeking a few minutes of rest before they return to the task at hand. Finally, we come to our designated spot, where several pop-up tents and plastic tables wait. We finish setting up just as the sun cuts through the sky, allowing daylight to creep in.

Within minutes, a line forms, and we spend the next two hours diligently filling plates for exhausted men and women. The atmosphere remains somber as they progress through the line. Their eyes reflect the harrowing realities they've confronted.

I'm loading up the empty trays in the van when Star appears in my peripheral.

"Tony," she says, placing a hand on my shoulder. "Someone's asking to speak to you."

I look to where she points and see Bill Miller, the FDNY chief, speaking with Owen. I don't need to hear what they're saying to know. "Please tell him I'll be over in a minute." I take my time finishing my task, doing my best to steel myself for the blow I'm about to be given.

Owen and Bill fall silent when they see me approaching.

"We found him." Bill's words knock the air from my lungs. "They're waiting for you to bring him out." We follow the commissioner to a waiting ambulance near the smoldering pile.

Rescuers momentarily pause their work and form two lines reverently flanking the path for their fallen brother.

Silence.

Stillness.

The only movement is the firefighters carrying the flag-adorned stretcher. They stop when they

come to where we stand.

"Anthony, it's my solemn duty to inform you that Battalion Chief Kameron Harlow perished while he was responding to the terrorist attack on September 11. Chief Harlow was heroically involved in the evacuation efforts in the North Tower and unfortunately perished in its collapse," Bill empathetically says. "On behalf of the FDNY, I'd like to express our deepest condolences on your loss."

"Thank you." The words come out in a strained whisper. My hand trembles as I reach out, placing it on the flag. "This can't be real," I murmur. "Please tell me this isn't happening."

"I'm so sorry, Tony," Owen says quietly.

"We need to take him now," Miller says.

"Don't let them do this." Tears blur my vision as I plead with Owen.

"You need to let them put him in the ambulance."

"I can't."

Owen puts his arm around me. "You don't have to do this alone."

"That's where you're wrong. I'm very much alone."

I force my legs to step back and watch as they carefully slide the stretcher into the back of the ambulance and close the doors. The sound echoes in the quiet space.

Motionless, with Star and Owen offering quiet support, I watch as the ambulance drives Kameron away. It isn't until they're out of sight that I silently turn and walk to our waiting SUV.

Anthony

DEATH—A STARK AND FINAL REALITY.

Grief is the unwelcome companion that lingers in its aftermath.

Death doesn't consider readiness. It steals loved ones away, leaving in its aftermath the heavy burden of grief.

The reality is, I knew he was gone the moment the tower fell. When several of his comrades were found in a pocket of safety, my heart naively grasped onto hope. Maybe Kameron was also trapped in a gap of steel and concrete, just waiting for rescue. I tried calling his cell phone over and over, praying he'd answer. But as the hours turned into days, a part of me recognized that wasn't going to be part of our story. Death stole Kameron from me.

Making the call to his twin sister, Kelsey, was one of the hardest things I've ever had to do. They were the only family each other had left. Maeve, their mom, passed away before their first birthday. She found out she had aggressive breast cancer early in her pregnancy. Her doctors gave her the impossible choice of treatment that required her to terminate the pregnancy or take her chances without treatment. She chose the latter. Unfortunately, by the time the babies were born, the cancer had spread and took her away from them a few months later.

Their father, Andy, was a wonderful man. After his wife passed away, he raised Kameron and Kelsey on his own. He never remarried. Andy frequently spoke of Maeve, and though I never had the chance to meet her, it felt as if I knew her through the vivid stories and memories he shared.

Kameron and his father were very close. Even when he came out as gay, Andy's support of his son never wavered. He stood by his son long before it was an acceptable thing to do. Andy lost friends and family members because of his outspoken support. Kelsey, Kameron, and I were by Andy's bedside when he took his final breath. I find comfort in the image of Andy and Maeve, arms wide open, ready to great Kam as he passed from this life to the next.

Kelsey met her husband, Birdie, on a trip to England shortly after Kam and I started dating. They had a whirlwind romance and married three months after they met. Much to Kameron's dismay, she permanently relocated to London. Kelsey and Kam have stayed close. We visit each other several times a year. Kameron and I had our tickets booked for a flight next month, and we were all set to stay with Kelsey and Birdie and eager to meet our first niece. Kam was so excited about becoming an uncle. Sadly, that, too, has been stolen from us.

Kelsey and Birdie have been trying to get to New York since everything happened, but with the flight disruptions, it's taken over a week for them to get here. I expect they'll be arriving any minute. Their flight landed over an hour ago. Birdie called to let me know they got their rental car and were on their way. I could hear their newborn daughter's cry in the background.

The hush of my apartment weighs heavily while I wait alone. I invited Owen and Star to stay, but they declined, wanting to give us privacy.

I'm checking the food in the oven when my doorbell rings, signaling their arrival. I quickly wipe my hands before going to answer the door. With a hesitant breath, I reach for the knob and slowly turn it to let them in.

Kelsey's eyes are red and puffy. When she sees me, a new wave of tears spills from her eyes as she falls into my outstretched arms.

"I'm so sorry, sweetheart," I say and kiss the top of her head. My eyes meet Birdie's worried gaze. "Come on inside." I keep my arm tightly around her shoulder as we walk into the living room.

"Please, say it's a lie," she whispers. "Tell me Kam is here."

"I wish I could." Seeing Kelsey shatter makes my battered heart break even more.

"We were watching it on the news, and I knew he'd be there, but..." Her words hitch with a sob. "I prayed that by some miracle, you two were out of town for your anniversary. Anything so he wouldn't have been there."

It's not the first time I wondered if I'd told him my plans before we left the house, would he have not taken the phone call? We would've been out of the country, and Kam would be here now.

"Kam was at the station when they got the call," I explain as we sit on the sofa. "He was one of the first on the scene."

"What was he thinking?"

"I don't have all the answers, but I can tell you what I know." She nods and wipes her eyes. "The phone lines were jammed, but Kam got a call out." My eyes close remembering the relief I felt when my phone rang, and I saw it was Kam. "He was in the North Tower, evacuating people."

"Did you tell him to get out?"

"I begged him to get out, but he said he couldn't make it." I recount some of our conversation without telling her too many details that would only upset her more.

"Was he scared?"

"I don't think so. He sounded peaceful."

The baby begins to stir in her father's arms. "I think Calliope would like to meet her uncle," Birdie says, trying to lighten the moment.

He passes the tiny newborn swaddled in a pale pink blanket to me, and I set eyes on the most perfect baby I've ever laid eyes on.

She steals my breath when she looks up at me, and I see a familiar amber gaze. "She has Kameron's eyes."

"She does." Kelsey rests her head on my shoulder. "I was always jealous of Kam's eyes." She laughs softly.

"Hello, Calliope," I say quietly. "I'm your Uncle Tony." I kiss her forehead and whisper, "Your Uncle Kameron would've just adored you.

"Now, because of those bastards, she'll never meet him," Kelsey says through her tears.

"We'll make sure she knows all about her Uncle Kam."

Kameron planned his funeral years ago. At the time, we'd argued about it, and I tried pulling the Dominant card, but he persisted. He understood the dangers of his job and insisted he make all the arrangements so that if the unthinkable ever happened, it would be something I didn't have to worry about. He didn't want a formal funeral in a church. All Kam ever wanted was a small gathering of his closest friends and family where we could celebrate his life.

Two nights after Kelsey and Birdie's arrival, we gather at *Flavour* for Kameron's memorial service. Both Kelsey and Birdie are well aware of our involvement in the BDSM lifestyle and are acquainted with our friends present tonight. Additionally, two surviving members from Kam's firehouse join us, flanking the side of the table where Kameron's remains rest. They vigilantly keep watch over Kam, positioned next to a photograph of him in full dress uniform and a solitary, flickering candle.

We're sitting down, about to start, when the door to the restaurant opens. Turning in my seat, I see Bill walking in with a very pregnant young woman I don't recognize. I walk over to greet them.

"I'm sorry for interrupting," Bill says quietly.

I look between him and the woman. "I'll get chairs for you and—"

"We can't stay, but I promised Adara I'd escort her here tonight." He touches the woman's elbow. "Adara, this is Anthony, Chief Harlow's partner."

"I'm sorry for interrupting the service," she says quietly. "But I had to speak to you."

"There's no need for an apology." I look down at the familiar item draped over her arm.

"I was at my desk on the eightieth floor in the North Tower when the first plane hit. At first, we were told it was a small accident, nothing to worry about, and that we should keep working. Shawn, my husband, worked in the South Tower. Thankfully, he was out of the office for a meeting, or he wouldn't be..." Her voice falters.

"He heard what happened and called me. Shawn said he didn't have a good feeling and that I should leave." She swipes at her tears. "I thought he was crazy, but I started getting my things together to leave. I wasn't in a hurry until I heard it. The sounds. I keep hearing them, even in my dream. I don't know if I'll ever be able to forget them." My hand extends to touch her arm, and in a tender exchange, she places her small hand over mine.

"The building shook. Pieces of concrete fell through the ceiling. That's when I knew it wasn't *nothing* like we were first told," Adara says with more certainty. Then she continues. "When the power went out, things quickly went from bad to worse. Everyone was screaming and crying. It was chaos, and I was certain we were all going to die." She looks up at me. "But I couldn't let that happen. I had to do whatever was necessary to get us out. So, I put my hand out to try to find the wall. Then I remembered I had a flashlight."

"Shawn works in telecommunications and insisted I have a brand-new fancy cell phone. He was so proud when he brought it home and showed me all the bells and whistles. I thought he was crazy." She laughs softly and shakes her head before becoming serious again. "But at that moment, I was so grateful for that silly little gadget. It lit my path, and I was confident I'd make it to safety."

"But I didn't make it. There was a loud roar." She closes her eyes momentarily as if reliving each detail. "It was so loud, and it wouldn't stop. Everyone started pushing and shoving. I did my best to stay against the wall to protect the baby." She gently caresses her round stomach. "In the commotion, I dropped my phone, and the light went out. I huddled in the corner as the building shook. From what I learned, it was the force of the South Tower collapsing. It still doesn't feel real," she says, her gaze lifting to meet mine.

"The air was filled with smoke, and it was dark, so very dark. All I could think was that I had to find that phone. I needed the light to get out. I searched for so long that suddenly, I realized it was quiet. There were no more voices. I was prepared to die there, alone, until I saw a faint light and heard a voice calling out. I yelled back, and Chief Harlow found me. As soon as he realized I was pregnant, he took off his oxygen and put it over my face. Then, he put his coat on me and strapped the tank on my back."

"We were going down the steps together until we met up with a police officer. Chief Harlow passed me to him and made him promise to get me out safely. Then, he disappeared." Her anguish deepens, and her tears fall faster.

"Thank you for sharing your story with me." I barely get the words out through my own tears.

"I needed you to know I'll never forget what he did for me— for us. And I wanted to be sure to return this to you." She hands me Kam's turnout coat.

The coat carries with it the unmistakable scent of smoke and Kam. "You'll never know how much this means to me." I hold it close to me, savoring the feeling of his presence. "How are you and the baby?"

"I inhaled a lot of smoke, so my doctor insisted I spend a few days in the hospital to monitor me and the baby. They said if Chief Harlow hadn't given me his oxygen, we wouldn't have made it. He saved our lives," she says softly. "But in doing so, he gave up his. I don't know if I'll ever be able to reconcile that."

"Kameron was a helper—a healer. He would get upset if I killed even the smallest insects. One day, I found a spider in our house. He got a sheet of paper and waited for that horrible creature to climb on it. Then he rode the elevator with it to deliver it to safety." I laugh softly at the memory. "Please know that Kameron would be happy to know his sacrifice ensured your survival. He wouldn't want you to question that."

"My baby is a boy," she says in a hushed tone. "With your permission, we'd like to name him Kameron."

The intensity of my tears prevents me from answering. This time, Adara is the one offering a calming touch. After a moment, I find my voice and say, "Kameron would be honored, and I am as well."

"Shawn and I will ensure our child knows the man he was named after," Adara adds. "He'll know that when everyone was running out, Chief Harlow ran back in. He's the true definition of a hero."

Before Bill and Adara leave, I introduce them to Kelsey. The women share a tearful embrace. Then I return to my seat, clutching Kameron's uniform tightly, as we prepare to say goodbye to Kameron.

The man I've loved and shared my life with.

The man who'll always have a part of my heart.

My beloved hero was taken far too soon.

Leopold

TWO YEARS. THAT'S HOW LONG I'VE BEEN LIVING— existing at Walking in Light. Ever since the day my parents caught me with Santiago. We had been best friends since elementary school, but as we matured, so did our feelings for one another.

My parents were supposed to be at church. Usually, I would've had to be there too, but I had a big project due at school, and I was excused from church that night. Ti was here helping me with it, except we got distracted. Neither of us heard their car pull into the driveway.

"We're home, boys," Mom says as she opens the door. "How the —" She freezes when she sees me on my knees with Ti's cock in my mouth.

It was the first time we ever did anything other than kiss.

"Mom." I jump to my feet and cover Ti as he hurries to close his pants.

My father came running to see what all the yelling was about. The only thing that saved Santiago from being physically thrown out of our house was the fact that he was sixteen, too, a minor. My father couldn't risk his perfect image being tarnished by being accused of assault.

Unfortunately, that courtesy didn't extend to me. After Ti left, Dad removed his belt and ensured I would not be able to walk or sit without pain for weeks to come. The following day, I was given a suitcase and told I had fifteen minutes to pack. My parents drove me to the Walking in Light Therapy Center, where I was admitted as a patient.

"This is for your own good," Mom cried as she kissed me good-bye. Dad wouldn't even look at me.

Standing in front of the full-length mirror, I tuck my dark blue button-down shirt and straighten the borrowed tie, ensuring my appearance leaves no room for one of David's punishments. Three days—that's all I have left until I turn eighteen and can sign myself out of the treatment center. I don't know where I'll go or how I'll get there, but I'll be damned if I stay in this hell hole any longer than I have to.

I glance at the clock, noting that I still have thirty minutes—ample time to review my notes. Last time, I missed what they considered *critical details*. The consequences are not something I wish to relive any time soon.

"Leopold," David says as he walks into my room. In this place, there's no such thing as knocking or privacy. "It's good to see you're taking today's assignment seriously."

"I am," I respond, attempting to conceal my intimidation as I lock eyes with his dark stare.

"As long as you don't fail, you will be one step closer to spiritual freedom," he assures. I nod, pretending I buy his line. "Come on, it's time."

I trail behind him, leaving my small room. Our dress shoes click-clack on the black and white checkered linoleum as we walk through the corridors to the meeting room where our daily group therapy sessions occur. He opens the door and motions for me to step inside. The room teems with other boys who are also patients undergoing *treatment*, therapists, and my family. I freeze, and David nearly walks into me.

"What's your problem?"

My eyes are locked on the people sitting in the first row. "You didn't tell me my parents and sisters would be here."

"Your parents and sisters are here." He leans in close and whispers, "If you screw up today, the consequences will be twice as bad as last time."

"Leopold, do you know why I've brought you here?" David, my therapist, asks.

"I forgot. I mean, I didn't," I stumble over my words. "I didn't say the right things."

David shakes his head and makes a tsking sound. "You aren't better yet," he says, lowering his voice. "The demon of homosexuality is still in you. But don't worry. I'm here, and I'll fix it," he says as he sticks electrodes to my skin.

"Please don't do this." Tears flow over my lower lid. "I promise I can do better."

"Why are you crying?" he snips. "Crying is not what a real man does. Is it, Leopold?"

I sniffle and try my best to stop the tears but fail. "No, sir." I know what he's going to do, and I don't think I can survive it again.

David pulls the screen down and turns the projector on. He passes me the clicker. "You remember what you have to do?"

"Yes."

The first image comes onto the screen. It's a heterosexual couple sitting on a park bench. I click, and the picture changes. This time, it's two men holding hands. I click quickly, knowing David will hit the shock button if I'm too slow. I do my best through several more pictures until there's one of a man sucking another man's cock. I hesitate a fraction of a second before hitting the clicker. David is watching my reactions carefully and hits the shock button. My body jerks, and I cry out from the force. The electricity is much higher than it's ever been.

"Real men are disgusted by those images, Leopold," he says snidely. "And they don't complain about pain."

In an effort to keep silent, I bite my lower lip and concentrate on not screwing up again. The hour-long session ends with my enduring a total of thirty shocks. At least half of which David gave me just to watch me writhe in pain. The electricity was up so high I had burns that took weeks to heal.

After Mr. Barry, the director, finishes his speech, I'm called to the front.

"Leopold has been part of our program longer than any other young man in our facility," Mr. Barry explains as I step onto the stage. "At the tender and impressionable age of sixteen, he had fallen deeper into the abomination of homosexuality than most of the other young men we have here." He forces a fake smile, glancing at the families with hopeful expressions. They all wish for this place to cure their sons and return them as perfect heterosexuals. "It's been a challenging journey, but we never give up. Do we, Leopold?"

"No, Mr. Barry," I respond respectfully, needing to get through this without incident.

"This evening, Leopold is taking the next step in his recovery," Mr. Barry announces, motioning for me to approach the podium. "Leopold will reflect on what he's learned during his stay with us." He turns to me. "It's all yours, son."

"Thank you," I say politely, placing my notebook in front of me and adjusting the height of the microphone. "Good evening, everyone." I glance up, but the room remains silent. "I was brought here two years ago after being caught in a homosexual act. Because of the expert treatment I've received at Walking in the Light, I've gained an understanding of the shame I cast on my family by my actions. My education here has taught me how a real man should behave. Today, I'm here to confess my wrongdoing." Looking up, I see my mother dabbing her eyes with a tissue.

"What happened was not a result of my upbringing. I allowed

worldly influences to lead me astray. My therapist has helped me to understand how I should talk and behave as a straight man. Homosexuality is something I will not fall prey to again."

David rises from his seat beside my father. "Do you, of your own free will, believe it is unnatural for a man to have sexual relations with another man?"

"Yes," I answer solemnly.

"Do you, of your own free will, agree when you leave this facility, you'll return to the loving care of your parents so they can continue to monitor you?"

I meet the stern stare of my father. "I do."

"Your speech was very well put together," David says, but the tone of his voice is off. My stomach sinks, realizing that things are about to go downhill for me. "However, you neglected to apologize for disgracing your parents."

"I apologized on our last phone call," I plead my case. "And I acknowledged they weren't at fault for my actions."

"I'm afraid that doesn't meet the requirements to graduate from our program," David says and motions to the row of newest arrivals. "You haven't set a very good example for the young men who are at the start of their healing journey."

Dropping my head, I give up trying to convince David of anything. It's pointless. I berate myself for being foolish enough to have hope. To believe that anything I said or did today would be enough to secure my ticket out of here.

"Mr. and Mrs. Wagner." David turns to address my parents and places his hand over his heart. "I wholeheartedly apologize for Leopold's failure tonight. I feel I must take responsibility for his failure. I will rectify this oversight by personally overseeing more intensive therapeutic measures to ensure his future success."

My family remains seated while the assembly is dismissed.

When we're the only remaining people, my father stands and approaches David. "We don't blame you for Leopold's resistance." He doesn't spare a glance at me. "We'll be praying for continued guidance." I resist the urge to roll my eyes, knowing it'll only make whatever David has planned worse.

"I'd like to take him right away. While this experience is still fresh in his mind. Although I understand if you'd like to speak with him in private before we leave."

Mom takes her place beside my father. "I'd like to speak with him."

"Darling," he says, putting his arm around her. "I think it's best to let him go with David."

"Thank you for understanding, Mr. Wagner." David turns to me. "Come over here, Leopold," he demands. "Say goodbye to your parents so we can go get started."

"Goodbye, Mom and Dad." I look to my sisters, who sit quietly on the pew. Arianna refuses to look at me while London watches intently.

"Thank your parents for coming."

"Thank you for coming," I parrot my reply.

"Please listen to what David tries to teach you." Mom reaches out and touches my cheek. "We'll see you soon."

I nod.

Dad takes her hand. "Let's go, girls," he says. My sisters stand and silently follow our parents out of the room.

"You're coming with me." David sneers, sending shivers down my spine. "Tonight's lesson is one you won't forget."

He grabs my wrist and pulls me behind him. David stops suddenly when London bursts back in.

"Can I help you?" David asks her impatiently.

London looks at him, her blue eyes filling with tears as she bats her eyelashes innocently. "May I please speak to Leo for a minute? I have something to give him." She holds up a book about avoiding worldly temptations. "I'd like to point out a chapter I feel could be particularly helpful for my brother," London says piously.

"Such a sweet young girl who clearly understands what we're trying to accomplish here. You'd be wise to listen to her." He smiles at London, and I cringe. David is pure evil. I don't want him anywhere near my little sister. "I'll give you a few minutes. It's imperative I start his session tonight as soon as possible."

"I understand. Thank you," she says sweetly. London waits until David is far enough down the hall to not overhear us. "There's a pre-paid card taped inside the bookmark I made. Use it to get yourself as far away from here as possible."

"What?"

"You're going to be eighteen. You can leave," London whispers and looks over her shoulder to be sure we're still alone. "I've been reading about this place online from other guys who were able to get out. They're pure evil." She takes my hand in hers. "I hate knowing you're here. Have they hurt you?"

"No." I squeeze her hand. "I don't know what you've read, but this is a great place." I lie. I can't tell her the truth and have her worrying about me.

She searches my eyes before continuing, "I highlighted some sentences and put a number by them. It's my phone number. When you get a phone, call me so I know you're okay."

London is five years younger than me, so we were never particularly close. She was only eleven when I was ditched here. I feel like she's a stranger to me and hate that I'm about to question her sincerity. But I have to know if this is a trap my father set up. "Did Dad put you up to this?"

"No," she says, taking a step back.

"Why are you doing this?" A tear slips down her cheek. I mentally chastise myself for doubting her.

"You're my brother and I love you." Footsteps get louder, and she leans in close. "Please take care of yourself."

I wrap my arms around her. "I love you, London."

"I love you, too."

"Leopold." David clears his voice. "Let's remember how a man should act."

"I've about had enough of the way you speak to my brother,"

London says, her hands on her hips, ready to go head-to-head with him.

"London, enough." I tug on her arm. "Thank you for the books. It was very kind. But it's time for you to leave now."

She glares at David for a few seconds before relaxing her posture. "Be sure to read that book. It has a lot of good information for men in your—" Her eyes flicker between David and me. "In your *situation*."

"I will."

"Have a good evening, Ms. Wagner."

As my sister walks out the double glass doors, I silently acknowledge it's the last time I'll ever see her. Staying out of her life is the only way I can protect her. If our father ever found out she helped me, he'd hurt her, and I can't let that happen.

David moves so close I can feel his warm breath on my neck. "Go put your book in your room and be at my office in five minutes."

Leopold

"STRIP," DAVID COMMANDS FROM BEHIND HIS oversized oak desk.

For a brief moment I consider not complying, but quickly course correct. The one time I fought back, I was bent over his desk and received twenty lashes with a whip. I couldn't sit or lie on my back for two weeks. That was all it took to learn that compliance is the only way to survive.

Once I remove my clothes, I go to sit in the usual chair in front of the screen, but David stops me. "We're not staying in here."

"What do you mean? Where are we going?"

He doesn't answer. Instead, he opens the door on the other side of his office. I always thought it led to a private bathroom, but I was wrong—so wrong.

When I don't move, he grabs my arm. "Let's go." He drags me through the door and over to what looks like some sort of torture device. It's meant to position a person on their knees while keeping their arms and legs restrained.

"What the fuck?" I mutter.

"We've tried this the easy way," David says as he pushes my chest against the black leather-like padding. My neck rests in an almost stockade-like device. With my legs spread, he attaches leather straps around them and then repeats the same with my arms. I'm exposed and vulnerable. "But you don't learn Leopold."

I assume I'm going to be whipped again, but why did he bring me in here? Why didn't he do it in his office like last time? Closing my eyes, I refocus my thoughts. Three days, I remind myself. That's all I have to survive.

After double-checking the restraints, David turns his back on me and walks across the room. I strain my neck to see what he's doing. Standing in front of a tall wooden cabinet, he pulls open a set of frosted glass doors. Inside are what look to be medical supplies. Small glass vials with labels on them that I can't read. Syringes. Needles.

"What's going on?" I ask and tug at the restraints.

Paying no attention to me, David picks up a brown-tinted vial and inserts a needle. He pulls back the plunger, fills it, and then flicks it a few times to get the air out. "You've left me no choice, Leopold."

My pulse quickens when he comes back toward me. "What's in there?"

"This?" He holds up the syringe. "It's a little something to make this lesson unforgettable."

"Get the hell away from me," I yell. "I don't consent to whatever you have in there."

David laughs sinisterly. "You don't consent? That's rich, considering you're tied up at the moment." He pierces my skin with the needle.

The liquid is cold as it's injected into my body. "What did you just give me?"

"You'll find out soon enough." David disposes of the used needle, turns off the lights, and walks out of the room.

Alone in the dark, I lose track of time. But I'm pretty sure, from my raging hard-on, that the injection contained a sexual performance drug. Sweat beads on my forehead from the fear of whatever evil game David's playing.

The door reveals a crack, allowing the light from his office to seep into the confined space. He walks to the front of me and looks down at the erection jutting out in front of me. "It seems the medication's working."

"You're sick."

"Another thing you seem to have backward, Leopold." He leans down closer to my face. "You're the one here because you don't understand where it's appropriate to stick your dick. But after this therapeutic intervention, I'm certain you won't be looking to put it anywhere for quite some time." He rubs his hands together. "Now, let's get started."

He opens another cupboard and takes out a silicone sleeve. "What's that?"

"This will provide some extra," he pauses. "Stimulation." He reaches out, taking my cock in his hand.

"Don't touch me," I protest. "You can't do this."

"That's where you're wrong. You can either hold still and let me put this on like a good boy, or I'll go back to my medicine cupboard for something to calm you down first. Either way, you lose."

I've never felt so helpless in my entire life. I'm restrained and at the mercy of this psycho. There's nothing else I can do other than watch him lubricate the silicone and slide it over my erection. David walks away and returns with electrodes he attaches to it. Then, he presses a button on the wall, and a screen unfurls from the ceiling. A projector overhead powers on, and an image of two naked men in bed appears.

"We're going to watch a little movie," he says as he sits across the room facing me. "Have you ever had sex with a man, Leopold?" I remain silent. "Tell me. Have you ever had a man's dick inside you?"

"You already know that answer." One of the parts of this so-called therapy has been disclosing not only every fantasy I've ever had but also every sexual experience. He knows I've never had sex.

"You're right," he says, jumping up from his seat. "I almost forgot the best part of tonight's session." David returns to the cupboard and pulls out a flesh-colored dildo. "It's not the real thing, but it should do the trick."

My stomach turns, and I'm thankful I haven't eaten in hours because what's in his hand is enormous. Despite my fear, my cock throbs, and a drop of pre-cum drips from the tip betraying me. David also notices, and that's when I feel what the tight sleeve around my cock does. A jolt of electricity flows through me, eliciting a cry of pain.

He opens the lube and squirts some onto his finger. "Ordinarily, I wouldn't be so kind as to make this comfortable for you," he says as he walks behind me. "But seeing as this is your first time, I'll go easy."

"Don't touch me." But it's too late. His finger is already breaching my opening. "What the hell do you think you're doing?"

"Helping you, Leopold." Another shock. "You'll thank me for this one day."

"That will never happen."

He withdraws his finger and, without warning, pushes the toy inside. My body stretches and

tears from the unwanted invasion. A metallic taste fills my mouth as I bite down on my lip to keep from making a sound. I refuse to give this monster any more ammunition.

"Now, we're ready," David says as he hits play and the screen comes to life.

It's the blond man's first time having sex with another man. David's taken my deepest secrets and is using them against me. Before I can think about it anymore, the dildo in my ass begins vibrating, which intensifies the arousal coursing through my body, courtesy of the drug he injected me with.

Sexual tension builds, both on the screen and in my body. The silicone wrapped around my cock begins massaging my erection. I close my eyes, trying to force my body to cooperate with me. This isn't right. I don't want this. So, why do I feel an orgasm building?

"Open your eyes, Leopold." When I don't listen, he hits the shock button again. But this time, he doesn't let it go, and the electricity continues to flow through the most sensitive area of my body until my eyes fly open. "That's better. You're learning the rules."

The men on the screen are touching. Kissing. Their actions, even though they're only playing to the camera, are consensual. The dark hair man lies on his back, his cock hard and ready, waiting for the blond who carefully lowers himself onto it. They moan in pleasure.

The blond man begins to move slowly as his partner strokes his dick. The dildo in my ass is turned up. My unwanted arousal builds as I'm forced to watch the screen.

"You like this, don't you, Leopold."

"Fuck you," I yell.

"Are you jealous that it's only a toy in you?" David pauses the movie. "Do you want my dick in your ass?"

"Stay the hell away from me, you sick bastard."

"That sounds like an invitation." David stands, and an erection tents his pants. He disappears behind me and pulls the dildo out. It hits the floor. "I'm going to fuck you. To take your virginity and make sure you never crave another man's cock in your ass."

He undoes his belt and zipper. The sound echoes in the small space.

"Get away from me." Although it's useless, I pull at the restraints as if my life depends on it. "Don't touch me."

David's hand digs into my hips as he impales me from behind, making me scream in anguish. He hits play and begins to move. He matches the pace of the men.

David grabs my hair, pulling my head back. "Keep your fucking eyes open, Leopold," he warns.

The blond man throws his head back as his cock spurts wave after wave of cum onto his partner's chest. The dark-haired man grabs the other's hips, taking control and increasing the intensity. David mimics him, digging his fingers into my hips as he pistons in and out of me. The room is filled with the sound of skin slapping against skin.

Despite my disgust, my balls draw up tight as my orgasm builds. Tears pour down my cheeks as I try to hold back, but it's useless. My cock pulses in waves. The electricity starts again, morphing the unwanted pleasure into agonizing pain. David thrusts hard and comes inside me with a deep growl. Everything happening at once is too much. My vision goes black.

Leopold

When I regain consciousness, I'm alone in the room. Somehow my cock is still excruciatingly hard. I try to move my arms and legs but am met with resistance. I'm still restrained—at David's mercy.

"Welcome back." David's voice plays through a speaker in the ceiling. "It's time to continue your lesson."

The words are barely out of his mouth when I feel the familiar vibration in my ass and around my cock. My body tenses at the unwanted sensations. Once again, the screen comes to life as the same movie begins to play from the beginning.

Hours. Days. Weeks. I have no idea how long he has kept me here. David appears every now and then, forcing me to drink, and then he injects me with more chemicals to ensure my body stays primed for more. I've lost track of how many times I orgasm against my will until I'm left trembling and exhausted.

The lights turn on abruptly, forcing me to squint from their brightness.

David enters the room and, without a word, pulls the toy from my ass, discarding it onto the floor, then moves to my front. "I'm impressed," he says as he pulls the silicone off my cock.

"You're still reactive. Don't worry. Once the medication is out of your system, this will go away." He moves in closer to whisper in my ear. "If it doesn't, I'll take care of it for you."

This sick bastard masquerades as a therapist. Someone who's vehemently anti-gay. But in reality, he likes men—boys. "You'll pay for this."

"I think you mean I do get paid for this." He disappears behind me. "He's ready. Come in."

Two men dressed in scrubs appear in front of me. I've never seen them before. David stands back as they carefully remove my restraints, and I nearly collapse into their arms. Holding me up by my elbows, I slowly walk back into the office, where a wheelchair waits. They help me sit and then cover me with a scratchy ivory blanket.

Silently, they wheel me to the infirmary unit, where I'm given a sponge bath and a hospital gown. Then I'm placed in a bed. One of the men starts an IV.

"I want to call the police," I say, my voice scratchy. "I need to report a rape."

"You're delirious from dehydration." He continues taping the catheter in place. "Once you get some fluids, you'll feel much better."

"No. I won't. David raped me," I yell, but he doesn't stop. "Do you hear me?"

"If your agitation continues, I'll be forced to give you a sedative." He pins me with his intense stare. "Am I going to need to do that?"

"No," I say quietly.

A short time later a doctor comes in. "You're going to be sore for a few days," he says after examining me. "But there's been no permanent damage done."

That's where he's wrong. David took something that didn't belong to him. He stole an experience that was supposed to be special and tarnished it with his evil.

"Do you have any questions?" the doctor asks, interrupting my thoughts. I shake my head. "Well then, happy birthday, young man."

"Birthday?" I ask, shocked by his statement. "How long was I in there?"

"You're asking how long your therapy session lasted?"

Is everyone in this place insane? "Yes." I correct myself. "How long did my *therapy* session last?"

"Four days," he says matter-of-factly. "You're one of our more severe cases. But I'm certain your therapist's work will serve you well. Our young men always leave here cured of their wicked ways."

"David's methods are very effective."

"I had no doubt you'd see reason." He writes something in my chart. "I'd like to keep you here overnight. Then you can return to your unit to continue your therapeutic recovery."

"Thank you. I look forward to it." I offer him a fake smile, knowing I have to be smart right now. I'm eighteen and can walk out of this place at any time. But I fear if they think I'm a flight risk, I'll be given that sedative. They need to believe I'm returning to treatment. "Is it possible for someone to bring the book my sister brought for me? I want to read it while I'm here. You know, continue my progress."

"I'll let the orderlies know."

My book arrives a short time later, and I mindlessly flip through the pages, pretending I'm taking in the information. What I'm really doing is plotting my escape.

The overnight staff is in, which means David is gone. I've been allowed to change into my sweatpants and a T-shirt. I'm given socks, but, per the rules, I'm not permitted shoes. Now, I have to wait and hope for the right opportunity.

Shortly after midnight, it does. A boy is brought in, screaming and completely freaking out. My heart aches for him, but right now, I have to focus on getting myself out. Once I make a police report, they'll come and shut this place down.

Taking a deep breath, I pull the IV from my arm. Blood spurts from my arm. I use the sheet to put pressure on it. As soon as it stops, I climb out of bed, slip the pre-paid card into my pocket, and stick the book in the waistband of my pants. I don't intend to contact London, but I won't leave evidence that she helped me.

Cracking open the door to my room, I check to be sure the walkway is empty and then quickly walk to the infirmary's exit leading to the residential unit. The halls are monitored, but with the smaller overnight staff busy with the behavioral incident, I don't meet any resistance.

There's one hurdle between me and the free world outside the main doors—the front desk staff. This is a locked unit. There's always someone stationed there. I have to hope they're reasonable and don't try to force me to stay or call for backup.

"Shouldn't you be in your room?" the woman asks when I approach. "It's past curfew."

"I'm signing myself out."

"I don't think—"

"I'm eighteen. You can't keep me here." I stand taller, hoping to show more confidence than I'm feeling. "The police know I'm coming. If you try to stop me, I'll make sure your name"—I look closer at her badge—"Cindy, is on the police report."

"Um. Of course." She starts typing. "What's your name so I can call your therapist. He has to do the discharge paperwork."

"That's not happening. Either give me something to sign or open the door," I say forcefully. "I'm leaving now."

"If I don't follow protocol, I'll lose my job."

"If you know what's good for you, you'll quit before it's too late." I glance from her to the door, my last obstacle before freedom. "Open the door."

She hesitates for a few long seconds before I see her hand move and hear the lock click. I don't hesitate. I push through and inhale my first breath of fresh air in two years.

I'm finally free.

Anthony

JANUARY 2002

Ninety-nine days. That's how long rescue and construction workers grappled with persistent hotspots flaring up and emitting plumes of smoke into the sky above Manhattan. Presently, Ground Zero resembles more of a construction site rather than the epicenter of a terrorist attack.

Work continues around the clock, removing the remaining piles of concrete and rubble. Earlier this week, they opened a viewing platform for anyone wishing to pay their respects. Several of my friends have gone and describe it as a moving and somber experience. I don't need to visit the site to relive the destruction and loss of that day.

Throughout Manhattan, weathered pictures of loved ones still dangle, torn and frayed. They're the constant reminder of the families whose loved ones' remains haven't been recovered. The unspoken hope of a miraculous reunion. Their prayers are a silent plea to discover their missing family member in a shelter or a hospital—a bewildered or injured survivor of this mass tragedy.

Yet, with each passing minute, that glimmer of hope fades. The harsh reality sets in, forcing more families to confront the same truth I've already come to terms with—their beloved is gone.

Their lives were snuffed out in a senseless act by a terrorist organization. It's the stark new reality we're all learning to live with.

Kelsey and Birdie stayed for two weeks after Kameron's memorial service. It was an honor to spend that time with them and Calliope. In the quiet stillness of the night, the newborn and I spent many hours together. Caring for Kameron's niece brought me comfort—a sense that he was near. I knew their time here was finite, but that didn't stop the tears I shed when we said goodbye.

The house has been too quiet since they left. This is the first time since that fateful day that I've been alone. I've heard the saying that silence is deafening, but I never fully understood it until now. Working in the food industry means I'm constantly bombarded with people and noise. Coming home at the end of a busy night was my sanctuary. The quiet was something I craved. Then, Kameron moved in. His presence filled each tiny crevice in both my home and my heart. The once comforting silence in my home has turned unwelcome, echoing the loss that now permeates every corner.

Although we weren't legally married, we were married in spirit and commitment. Our bond extended past the romantic into our unique lifestyle, where Kameron was my devoted submissive. The closeness we shared was unparalleled. His absence has left a gaping hole in my life. My home is once again quiet, but it's unwelcome.

In the days following the attack, I lived in a constant state of denial. It was unfathomable that my Kameron died—a mistake. A nightmare I'd soon wake from. Then, they pulled Kam's body from the rubble. After the initial shock, I was angry. How dare Kameron leave me? We were supposed to spend forever together. We didn't have enough time.

More than one night was spent bargaining with God or any other higher power who would listen to somehow bring Kameron back to me. When that didn't happen, I felt myself sinking into an abyss. Kam's memorial service was a poignant mix of profound grief and the brightness of hope. I was forced to say goodbyes to the man I loved beyond words, but I also met Adara.

Listening to her recount how Kameron selflessly gave her his lifeline, his oxygen, didn't surprise me. Kameron's instinct to prioritize others went beyond his professional duty—it was intrinsic to his character and the reason behind his chosen career. As angry as I might've been at him for going against all his training and giving up his source of oxygen, it all melted away as I witnessed Adara caressing her stomach.

At that moment, I realized that Kam saved not only Adara's life but also the life growing inside her. The knowledge that this unborn child would bear Kameron's name brought a deep sense of peace, offering the reassurance needed to begin the process of moving forward.

It's been four months since I've stepped foot in the empty space that should be my restaurant—the last place I saw *amore mio*. *Italiano Desiderio* started as my dream but quickly became a shared dream. Kameron had a hand in every decision, from the interior design to the menu. Which is why I have to continue on. The loss of Kameron and many others on that tragic day has cast a shadow of grief over everyone in my circle. The impact of the tragedy was felt far and wide, leaving no corner of the world untouched.

My loss is not greater than that of anyone else's. I've spent too much time at home wallowing in self-pity. Whether I fully embrace it or not, the time has come to put a smile on and get back to work. I arrive early at my soon-to-be restaurant and take a few moments to myself.

I'm lost in a daydream when the door opens unexpectedly. "I didn't mean to startle you."

"It's all good."

"You must be Mr. Genovese," he says.

I smile and extend my hand. "Please, call me Tony."

"I'm Al. It's a pleasure to meet you." I was tied up at the club when he first came out to take measurements. I'd sent Margot, my childhood friend and interior designer, to oversee that day. So this is our first official meeting. "Please accept my condolences on your loss."

"Thank you. Shall we sit and discuss how we proceed?" I ask, motioning to a table and chairs left over from the previous business.

Over the next hour, Al details all of the permits that have been pulled, a start date for the demolition, and a timeline for completing the construction part of this project.

"Barring any unforeseen complications, we should have everything on our end completed in ten weeks," Al explains.

"This has been so long in the making I can hardly believe it's finally happening," I murmur, part of me still not wanting to do this alone.

My hand trembles as I put pen to paper. The absence of a line for Kameron's signature isn't lost on me. It pains me to move forward without him, but I can almost hear him telling me to keep going.

"My crew and I will be here at seven am," Al says as he gathers his papers.

I reach into my pocket. "For you." I hand him my extra key.

"Thank you, mister—Tony."

After we finalize a few details, I see Al out and lock up.

The afternoon wanes, and the sun casts a low glow in the January sky. Despite the cool air, I choose to cover the mile to Fire and Ice on foot. I've been carrying Kameron's collar with me since the night I was supposed to give it to him. Tonight, surrounded by the love and support of my chosen family, I'll pay tribute to the commitment Kam and I once shared.

Anthony

It's still quiet in the club when I arrive. I avoid the area set up for us and instead make a beeline for the café.

"How's everything coming in here?" I ask the small kitchen staff who are hard at work. Lawrence, the sous chef, is at the stove working on what looks like the pasta.

"The food will be ready in twenty minutes." Marcy, our very talented chef, assures me.

"Did the champagne arrive?" On one of our visits to see Kam's sister, we attended an exclusive wine tasting. Kam fell in love with Armand de Brignac Rosè. We toasted with that champagne after we exchanged vows.

"Yes, Chef. It's chilling as we speak."

"Where is the—"

"Tony." Marcy puts her tiny hand on my arm. "Your guests are arriving." I glance out of the kitchen window. Brandon and Alex are just arriving. "Go out and greet them. I have everything under control," she reassures me.

"Okay," I finally concede.

Star and Owen closed Fire and Ice to everyone other than the small group of my close friends so we could pay a special tribute to Kameron. A large round table sits on the main floor of the club. It's already been set for dinner. In the center is a glass box that will hold Kameron's collar.

For the past few months, I've carried it with me, afraid that if I let it go, I'd lose my final connection to him.

"I'm glad you could make it tonight." I shake Alex's hand.

"I wouldn't be anywhere else."

"Thank you for coming." I turn to Brandon and extend my hand, but he pulls me in for a hug instead.

"Anything for you," he says, and I hear the emotion in his voice.

While everyone chats, I step off to the side.

Owen comes over to where I'm standing. "How are you holding up?"

"I'm fine." I offer him the smile I've gotten good at showing others. "Is Scarlett here?" I ask, hoping to distract him.

"She's in the back with Star. They'll be right out."

"Great. I'm going to go check on Marcy."

I attempt to make an escape, but Star stops me on the way. "I believe everyone's here. Are you ready to get started?"

"I was going to check on the food."

"Marcy's on top of it," she says reassuringly.

"Right." I nod and walk with her to the table. "Tonight, we're gathering to honor Kameron's devotion to our Dominant/submissive relationship. The night before Kameron passed away, I'd made plans to not only celebrate our anniversary but also to ask him to accept my collar. Unfortunately, he was called in to work. When he called me and told me he wasn't going to make it out, I asked him to wear it, and he accepted." A sharp pain stabs my chest, and I momentarily can't take a breath. "I've carried it with me since that day. I couldn't let it go."

"When Owen and I had lunch last week, we discussed my dilemma. He asked if I'd be willing to display the collar at the club to honor Kam. I immediately said yes." I take a deep breath, composing myself. "Tonight isn't meant to be another tearful sendoff, but rather an evening to remember the man we all knew and loved. And to honor Kameron's devotion to our Dominant/submissive relationship. Kameron loved this place, and he loved each of you." I look around the table at my chosen family and silently chastise myself as I blink back the tears that are threatening to fall.

There are several chuckles as plates of mozzarella sticks are brought out. Kameron's preferences in food ranged from sophisticated five-star dining to simple microwave meals.

"It didn't matter where we went," Brandon says. "Kam always searched the menu for cheese sticks. If they weren't on there, he'd offer to pay the kitchen extra to make them."

"Do you remember when we surprised him at the fire station?" Scarlett asks.

"How could I forget?" Owen laughs.

Two years ago, Owen made a mozzarella stick cake for Kam's birthday. It looked incredibly realistic.

"Poor Kam was almost in tears when he picked one up and took a bite." She laughs. "I felt so bad that after we left, I baked a whole tray full and brought them back to the fire station."

After our Caesar salads, Marcy and Lawrence serve the penne alla vodka.

"I'll never forget the first night you brought Kameron here," Alex says. "You sat front and center with him for the knife play scene Kam was obviously not expecting."

"I had looked at the wrong date and thought there was supposed to be a Shibari demonstration," I recall, a smile tugging at my lips.

"That explains why his jaw dropped when the scene started. I was waiting for him to sprint out the door," Brandon adds.

"To be honest, so was I," I say, and we all share a laugh. "Yet somehow that night, after we left, he lowered to his knees and asked to submit to me."

Over the course of the next two hours, everyone takes turns sharing their favorite and often comical memories of Kameron.

The conversation turns more serious when Star says, "Witnessing Kameron's submission was breathtaking. Too often a man's submission is viewed as a sign of weakness, but that's rarely the case," she explains and glances to the man at her side. "It takes a strong person, regardless of gender, to gift another something so precious."

"The connection we shared was indescribable." I reach out and stroke the leather collar.

Each of us at the table falls into a heavy silence, the air thick with unexpressed emotions.

"Are you ready?" Owens asks quietly.

"I am." His firm grip on my arm conveys a silent message of support.

"It's clear from all the stories tonight that Kameron has left an indelible mark on everyone's lives and our community as a whole." I rise from my seat and lift the collar from the table. Owen stands beside me.

"Star and I are honored that Tony has agreed to allow us to display Kameron's collar," he says, clearing his throat. "It will forever symbolize the commitment Anthony and Kameron shared. The love we were all privileged to watch blossom." Owen lifts the lid, opening the box.

"Thank you for your gift of submission and your love," I whisper as I set the leather band onto its silver velvet resting place, then carefully close the box.

"We." Owen motions between Star and himself. "Had this lock made. There's no key signifying a bond that can never be broken."

Despite my resolve not to cry all evening, I lose the internal struggle. Quiet tears stream down my face as I hold the silver lock, bearing the engraved words, *Kameron Harlow—Forever in our hearts.* With trembling hands, I secure the lock.

After inhaling deeply, I lift my face and address my friends,

"Please join me for a toast," I request, raising my glass. Everyone gets to their feet. "To the man who filled my life with excitement, joy, unwavering support, and, most importantly, unconditional love. My heart will forever be yours. Until we meet again, *amore mio.*"

Leopold

I FIND MYSELF IN SAN DIEGO, A CITY ENTIRELY NEW TO me. The soles of my socked feet are throbbing as I wander the dimly lit streets, mentally marking locations of stores that might have reasonably priced shoes and an affordable spot for breakfast come morning.

Exhausted, I walk until my legs can no longer carry me. Collapsing onto a park bench, I curl up, drawing my limbs close in a protective cocoon. As my eyes shut, the world blurs, and I slip into a restless sleep, shadows dancing on the periphery of my consciousness. Grateful, I welcome the rising sun for bringing its warmth to my body and opening a new chapter in my life.

The streets look different in the daylight, and it takes me a little while to find my bearings and remember where the second-hand store is. People sharing the sidewalk with me shoot disgusted looks my way as they give me a wide berth. Stopping, I look at my reflection in a store window.

My hair is mussed, poking in all directions. I pick a stray leaf out of it. The T-shirt I was given is too big for my frame and hangs loosely off my shoulder. My baggy sweatpants have torn knees, and I'm wandering shoeless. With tears blurring my vision, I look around and am relieved when I spot the second-hand store at the end of the block. When I step inside, I almost expect to be thrown out. I'm thankful the woman working the checkout is busy with another customer, allowing me to sneak past.

Making my way to the back of the store where the shoes are set up, I search the racks for something that's my size. Several minutes later, I find a used pair of Nike sneakers. They're well-worn, and the laces are tattered, but beggars can't be choosers. Passing on the offered bag, I hurry outside and slide my feet into my new-to-me shoes.

My next stop is a fast-food place a few doors down, where I grab a bacon, egg, and cheese bagel, a hashbrown, and an orange juice. Finding a cozy corner booth, I slide into it. It's been two years since I've tasted anything besides cafeteria food. My eyes close as I savor the taste of the processed sandwich.

Stepping back into the warmth of the day, my nerves shift into overdrive as I contemplate where I need to go now. I've been waiting since shortly after I arrived at Walking in the Light for today—my opportunity to make a police report against David and get that hall of horrors shut down.

The day has barely begun, and I'm already exhausted. Thankfully, the police station is only a few blocks away. I walk through the sliding glass doors into the air-conditioned lobby and make my way to the desk where a uniformed officer is stationed. "Can I help you?" he asks as he looks up.

"I'd like to file a police report," I say, my voice cracking, betraying my nervousness.

"Have a seat." He points to a small sitting area behind me. "Someone will be right with you."

My slightly too big shoes scuff on the linoleum floor, making a loud squeak. I look over my shoulder, expecting to be scolded for the noise, but the officer hasn't looked up from whatever he's writing. Carefully, so as not to press my luck, I continue the short walk to the outdated upholstered chairs and sit. My leg bounces nervously while I wait to be called back.

After a brief wait, an older man emerges. "Are you the one looking to file a report?"

"Yes, sir." I stand and cross the room.

"This way." He motions for me to go through the door ahead of him. "We're going to interrogation room three. It's on your left." My heart races as we walk down the narrow hallway and into the room. "Have a seat." The officer opens a brown metal filing cabinet and searches through the hanging folders.

The room is sparsely furnished, with only a small rectangular table surrounded by four plastic folding chairs. I walk around, sit facing the door, and wait for the officer to join me.

"I'm Lieutenant Pierce," he says as he sits across from me and clicks his pen. "Let's start with your name."

"Leopold Wagner."

"Address?"

"I don't have one," I mumble under my breath, the confession delivered in a low tone.

"Pardon me?"

"I don't have an address." Embarrassment floods through me, and I glance over the officer's shoulder at the door, debating if I should leave.

"Are you homeless, young man?" Lieutenant Pierce's tone is compassionate.

Beneath the table, I wring my fingers nervously in my lap. "Yes, sir," I affirm quietly.

Setting his pen down, he folds his hands. "Do you have any family in the area I can help you get in touch with?"

"My family and I are no longer in contact."

"I see," he says and flips to the next page. "What's the nature of the crime you wish to report?"

"I was raped." I discreetly fold my hands on the table, attempting to conceal the tremors.

"Would you mind if I brought in one of my colleagues to assist with this report?"

"Um." I bite my lip and shrug. "I guess not."

Lieutenant Pierce stands, his chair squeaks loudly on the floor. "Can I get you anything to eat or drink?"

"May I have a water?"

He smiles kindly, saying, "Sure. I'll be right back." Then he steps out and leaves me alone.

My foot taps nervously beneath the table while I silently review the story I practiced while I was in the infirmary. Several minutes later, Lieutenant Pierce returns with a female officer.

"This is Detective Ridley," he says and motions to the woman beside him before passing me a plastic bottle of water. "She's specially trained to help with reports of sexual violence."

"Thank you." I take the offered drink, unscrew the cap, and take a drink. The ice-cold water soothes my dry throat.

"First, please call me Julie," the detective says as she sits in the chair next to the Lieutenant. "Do you prefer to be called Leopold or Leo?"

"Leo, please."

"Okay, Leo," she responds, her smile radiating warmth. "We have a lot of questions to get through," Julie explains. "I know this process can be difficult, so if you need a break at any point, just say the word. Okay?" I nod. "Where would you like to start?"

"I'm not exactly sure where to begin."

"Are you able to tell me when or where the assault occurred?" she asks patiently.

"It all happened at the Walking in the Light Therapy Center," I say a little louder, finding my voice. "The abuse has gone on for two years. I was raped four days ago."

"What are you able to tell me about what happened?"

Over the next few hours, I tell the officers everything I remember, starting with the very first *therapy session,* where I was repeatedly held under water as they tried to cleanse me of my *sins.*

At one point, Lieutenant Pierce excuses himself. When he returns, he has a tray of pizza. "We've been at this a long time," he says, passing out paper plates and napkins. "I thought we could all use something to eat." My mouth waters looking at the delicious round pie on the table, but I don't dare make a move.

"It's okay, Leo," Julie says, pushing the box toward me. "Help yourself."

I hesitate for another second before tentatively reaching out. Jule nods, encouraging me to keep going.

They try to keep the conversation light while we eat, but I'm anxious to tell the rest of my story. I want this over as soon as possible. They listen carefully and ask several questions, trying to get as many details as I can give.

"When were you discharged?" Lieutenant Pierce asks.

"I wasn't discharged," I say and explain how I was able to get out while the nightshift was busy.

"When did you turn eighteen?" Julie asks.

"Yesterday."

She sits up and asks, "So, this happened when you were still a minor?"

"Yes, ma'am."

"At the risk of sounding callous," Lieutenant Pierce says, "I do want to wish you a Happy Birthday."

"Thank you."

"I think we have enough information," he says, tapping the papers on the table.

"Leo," Julie says, a serious tone in her voice. "I'd like to ask if you'd consent to having an exam and rape kit done."

"Even though it happened days ago?"

"Ideally, the exam would be done sooner," she admits. "There's still the chance we could get some DNA evidence to support your claim."

"Um." I chew on my bottom lip. "If you think it would help."

"It's a long shot, but I think it's worth doing."

"Okay, then."

She offers me an empathetic smile. "Leo," she says, reaching out to touch my hand. "What you've done here is very brave."

"I guess." I shrug and look down at my lap.

"Before you leave, I'd like to discuss your living arrangements," she continues. "Lieutenant Pierce explained that you're homeless." I nod, embarrassed by my current situation.

"We can help with that."

"You can?" I ask, my head popping up.

"There's a local program, Safe Haven, that offers transitional housing to young adults in the LGBTQ+ community," she explains. "While you're with them, they'll help you with finding a job and a permanent place to live as well as provide you with the mental health services you'll need as you recover from this trauma. Does that sound like something you'd be willing to try?"

The past two years, confined in a supposedly safe place, have left me wary of diving straight into another one.

"I understand your hesitation," Julie says. "I can personally vouch for Ramiro and the Safe Haven program. The rest of the Special Victim's Unit and I personally oversaw the organization of this program. Ramiro works closely with us." She pauses, searching my face for a reaction. "The doors are not locked there."

"I can leave if I don't like it?" I ask.

"Yes," she says. "I can take you there and wait while you have the exam done."

My hand instinctively covers my mouth to stifle a yawn. Despite the lack of physical exertion, mentally reliving the events takes its toll. Add to that a night spent on a park bench, and I'm ready to sleep for a week. "Okay," I concede.

Leopold

I'VE BEEN AT SAFE HAVEN FOR THE PAST MONTH AND finally feel like I'm letting my guard down and settling in. Julie checked in on me multiple times during my early days here to make sure I was settling in okay. It was a reassuring experience to spot a familiar face amid so many strangers. Safe Haven's been a sanctuary while I work towards getting on my feet and figuring out my next steps.

Within a few days, Ramiro, the program's leader, helped me find a job at a small bodega. It's not glamorous, but it's a steady paycheck.

Today, I have the day off and have spent it in my room, diligently studying for my GED test scheduled for next month. Despite the claims of Walking in the Light having a high-quality educational program for its residents, the reality is starkly different. Two hours each day were designated for *school,* and I use that word very loosely. It was more important to the powers that be that we attended their brainwashing sessions. It ensured we all remained dependent on them—stuck.

"Hey, Leo." Ramiro pops his head into my doorway. "Julie is here."

"I didn't realize she was coming today." There's a rush of both nervous energy and excitement within me.

"I'm assuming she has an update," he says with a hopeful smile. "She's in my office waiting for you."

"Thanks. I'll be right out."

"I'll let her know." He raps his knuckles on my doorframe before disappearing down the hall.

Closing my book, I neatly put it away before scrutinizing my appearance in the mirror. My heart thuds with anticipation as I walk towards Ramiro's office. Julie stands when she sees me round the corner.

"I hope I didn't come at a bad time," she says.

I crack my knuckles nervously. "Not at all."

"Do you have a few minutes to talk?"

"Sure."

"It's a beautiful day. Are you up for a walk?" she suggests.

I follow her outside and across the street to the park. We walk in companionable silence, listening to birds chirping in the trees. Deciding I can't take the suspense any longer, I ask, "Has there been any progress on my case?"

"That's what I came to talk about. A few things have transpired," she says, motioning to a nearby bench overlooking a fountain, and we both sit. "David Lewis and his attorney came in last week for questioning. We also had one of our detectives visit the treatment center. Everything we collected was sent to the prosecutor's office." She takes a deep breath before continuing. "There wasn't enough evidence, so they closed the case."

I'm taken aback. "What do you mean, closed the case?"

"The charges you made against Mr. Lewis have been dropped."

"Dropped?" I face her squarely. "So, he gets off the hook for what he did to me?" I question, raising my voice. "What about the rape exam? They saw the tears."

"We talked about the difficulty with the exam since so much

time had passed," she says calmly. "There was no DNA evidence to substantiate your claim. After interviewing Mr.—"

"Stop." I hold up my hands, interrupting her. "Let me guess. David convinced you he's an upstanding therapist doing everything possible to help the troubled gay kid."

"I can't divulge what was said during his questioning."

"Of course. We need to protect *David's* rights," I say sarcastically.

"I know you're upset," she says.

"Upset? That's an understatement. David raped me." My voice resonates loudly enough to draw the attention of passersby. "He raped me," I add, lowering my tone. "And he's going to get away with it."

"I'm very sorry, Leo. There's nothing more we can do right now."

"I guess that's it, then." I stand.

"Leo, sit down, please. Let's talk about what happens next," Julie encourages me. "I have the name of a good trauma therapist. She specializes in cases like yours." She reaches into the pocket of her slacks.

"No thanks. I've had enough of *helpful* therapists." I rock on my heels, needing to get away. "Thanks for trying." I shrug and start walking.

"Leopold, please," she calls after me, but I wave her off and hurry away.

Hours pass as I walk, and it's only after sunset that I come to a standstill outside *Prism*, an all-ages club for the LGBTQ+ community. Some of the guys from Safe Haven like to hang out here. Several times, they invited me along, but I didn't feel ready.

Other than the short-lived relationship I had with Santiago,

I've never been in a relationship, and it's only been a little over a month since I was raped by my therapist. My life has been on hold, waiting to see David on the witness stand and hearing the hammering of the judge's gavel pronouncing his prison sentence. It was supposed to fix the pain—chase away the nightmares. But now there's nothing to heal what's broken inside me.

I swing the club's door open, only to be stopped at a security check point.

"ID," the burly bouncer demands.

Reaching into my back pocket, I pull out my wallet and hand the guy my picture identification. Eventually, I'll get my driver's license, but this is a start.

A bright yellow band is affixed to my wrist, identifying me as under twenty-one and unable to drink. Something I don't really care about. My goal is to get lost in a sea of faces. To pretend, even if just for one night, that I'm not some screwed-up gay kid who everyone thinks needs to be fixed.

I grab a seat at a table in a dimly lit back corner. The thump of the bass is hypnotic and distracts me from the jumbled thoughts in my head.

"Is this your first time at *Prism*?" a server asks.

"It's that obvious?"

"I've worked here for a long time and am familiar with most of the regulars," he says, a friendly smile accompanying his words. "I'm Nick."

"It's nice to meet you, Nick. My name's Leo."

"Here's our menu." Nick hands me a cardstock menu. "Take a few minutes to look it over. You can't go wrong with anything on it."

Nick leaves me to decide what to order when I spot *him*. He's tall and broad-shouldered, with jet-black hair that hangs past his shoulders. His emerald-green eyes meet mine, and something within me stirs to life. I quickly avert my gaze, not wanting to be the wierdo staring with his mouth hanging open. But even without looking up, I feel his presence getting closer.

"How is it a man who looks like you is here by himself?" he asks in a deep, gravelly voice.

"I'm um," I stumble over my words. "Just getting a quick bite to eat."

"Mind if I join you?" He motions to the empty chair across from me.

"Sure," I answer shyly.

"I've never seen you here before. Do you go to the university?"

"Me? No." I'm feeling all kinds of flustered by this man. "I was just in the neighborhood. Looking for..."

He raises an eyebrow. "Looking for?"

I'm at a loss for how to respond. I don't know what I started out looking for, but I know what I found.

Him.

An unfamiliar electricity courses through my body. The sexy stranger studies me while I search for the right words.

"This place is too loud," he says, leaning closer. "How about we get out of here and go someplace we can talk."

Setting the menu on the table, I meet his penetrating stare. "Go somewhere? I don't know you." As soon as the words are out of my mouth, I realize how juvenile they sound and want to hide under the table.

He chuckles. "That's something easy to fix. I'm Krew."

"Leo."

"Now, we know each other." His tongue wets his lower lip. "I have an apartment a few blocks away. We can—"

Nick returns, interrupting us. "Are you ready to order?"

"He isn't going to be ordering," Krew says, his eyes never leaving mine. "I'll take care of him at my place.

My dick springs to life at his innuendo.

"I wasn't asking you." Nick turns to me. "Leo?"

"Thanks for the menu." With my eyes locked onto Krew's, I pass the menu back to my server. "But I won't be needing it."

Nick narrows his eyes at Krew before addressing me, "I don't think that'd be a good idea."

"I think you need to mind your own business, Nicky," Krew says as he sits back and crosses his arms over his broad chest.

"Leave him alone, Krew." Nick turns his attention back to me. "You seem like a good kid, Leo. You don't need to get mixed up with someone you don't know."

Krew and Nick watch me expectantly. I'm at a pivotal moment—a crossroads. Should I play it safe, acknowledging the unspoken warning in Nick's tone, or embrace the instant attraction I feel towards Krew?

"I appreciate your concern," I say to Nick. "Krew and I were supposed to get together earlier, but he was running late." I glance at Krew, who curls his lip in a smile. "I was going to order while I waited for him, but plans are changed now."

Krew pushes out his chair and stands. "Let's go, Leo." He offers me his outstretched hand.

Standing, I place my hand into the handsome stranger's and allow him to lead me away.

Leopold

Krew tightens his grip on my hand as he guides me away from Prism. Though not well-acquainted with the city, I remember Ramiro's caution about staying out of the East Village, particularly after dark. My heart races as we turn down a dimly lit side street. We stop in front of a three-story brown brick building, its first-floor windows secured with bars.

"This is where you live?" I ask hesitantly.

"It is." He pulls the solid steel door open and steps aside. "Unless you've changed your mind," he says, raising an eyebrow.

Summoning courage, I pull my shoulders back and respond, "I haven't."

"Good," he says, his voice tinged with desire. "Up the steps, first door on the left."

"How long have you lived here?" I ask, attempting to make conversation.

"About four years." He stops at another steel door that has a peephole. Unlike the exterior door that had a lock and key, this one has a black box where Krew punches in a code. A locking mechanism clicks, and Krew opens the door. He enters first, and I follow suit. As soon as I step across the threshold, Krew turns around, closing the door behind me and trapping me against it with his arms.

Leaning into me, his lips meet mine, and his tongue seeks entrance. Instead of relaxing into the kiss, I flinch and resist.

Krew pulls back and studies my face. "Did I get this wrong?"

"No. It's. I—"

"You're not into men?" he asks.

"I am," I answer quickly.

"Are you with someone?" He takes a step back. "I'm into a hell of a lot, but I'm not about to be someone's side piece."

"There's no one else," I admit, looking up to meet his intense gaze. "This is unfamiliar territory for me. I've never just gone home with someone."

"Well then," Krew says, pressing himself against me. "I'm more than happy to be the first."

This time, when his lips meet mine, I welcome him. His kiss is demanding and rough. His hard cock presses against my stomach. I was afraid, after what David did to me, that my body wouldn't respond, but that's not the case. My dick is hard and strains against the zipper of my jeans.

In a bold move, I reach down and grab his cock through his pants.

"I want you to suck it," he says, and although I'm surprised by his command, my hands move to his zipper. I push his pants down and lower to my knees. Taking his cock in my hand, I stroke it gently. It's much bigger than I anticipated. My experience with blow jobs is limited to that one night with Santiago, and that didn't end well.

Hoping not to embarrass myself, I open my mouth and wrap my lips around the tip. I try to take all of him in but gag on his length. My movements are erratic and sloppy as I repeat the motion. Krew threads his hand in my shaggy blond hair. With a firm grip, he pushes me all the way down so his cock is deep in my throat and holds me there. My eyes water, and my vision blurs. Grasping at his thighs, I struggle to get free.

He pulls me back and watches as I cough and struggle to catch my breath. "Have you ever sucked a man off before?" he asks, and I shake my head. One side of his mouth cracks up in a smile. "Are you ready to learn how to please me, Leo?"

"Yes."

"Good boy," he praises me. "Now, open your mouth and relax." He thrusts his dick into my mouth, and I suck. "Take it all," he commands, grabbing my hair and pushing me down until my face is against his groin. I gag, and he laughs.

Over and over, he guides my head up and down his length until I start to relax under his control.

"That's my boy," he says, looking down at me with lust-filled eyes, and I feel my face flush. "Take it out and show me how much you like it."

I pull his cock out of my mouth, stroking him with one hand while the other massages his balls.

"Mmm. Just like that." He closes his eyes.

Seeing him enjoy my ministrations makes me feel powerful. I run my tongue along his slit, tasting his salty pre-cum then circle his velvety tip before taking him in all the way down my throat. He groans as I suck him.

"You're a natural," he says. "Are you ready for me to fuck your face for real now?" I nod. Krew grabs me by the back of my neck, holding me tightly as his cock slams against the back of my throat with each thrust. Saliva runs down my chin as he pumps in and out.

I gag and choke on his cock, but he keeps going. "Take it," he says through gritted teeth. My eyes water as fucks my face. "You like this, don't you?" My hand moves between my legs and rubs my hard cock through my pants. "Do not touch yourself," he commands.

I grab his thighs to steady myself as he thrusts harder and faster. "I want you to look at me while you suck my dick," he says, and my eyes shoot up to his. "I'm going to cum." Thrust. "You're going to swallow everything I give you," he roars as he slams to the back of my throat and empties himself. He pulls out halfway and strokes his cock a few more times, ensuring I take every last drop.

"Now, lick me clean." I do as I'm told, licking his salty and musky cum off his dick and balls. "You're a good little cocksucker," he says as he tucks himself back into his pants. "I'm going to put a frozen pizza in the oven."

Krew walks away, leaving me on the floor. I sit back on my heels and wipe a mix of spit and cum from my chin. Once I've caught my breath and am confident I can stand, I make my way across his apartment and ask, "Can I use your bathroom?"

"Down the hall," he says without turning around. "It's the only door on the right."

Silently, I walk away from him down a dimly lit hallway. There's an open door on each side. I peek my head into the room on the left. It's a cramped bedroom with white walls. There's a full-sized bed with no headboard. The blankets are in a sloppy pile. Across from it is a dresser with clothes hanging out of several drawers. I don't want to linger too long, so I back out and go into the bathroom right across the hall.

Like the bedroom, it's not well kept. The old tub is yellowing and has chips broken off it. The frosted shower doors are half off their track. I rinse off my hands and face in the lavatory-style sink. I look around for a towel to dry my face but don't find any.

Gripping the edge of the sink, I stare at my reflection in the cracked vanity mirror. That was my first consensual sexual act. I always imagined it would be different, more romantic. Maybe my expectations for a relationship with another man are unreasonable?

Krew is the epitome of drop-dead gorgeous with a side of danger. He's a man who knows what he wants and isn't afraid to go after it. That kind of confidence is sexy as hell. How he took charge and showed me exactly how to please him made me feel powerful. It was after that things were different than I'd imagined. I guess this is where I need to man up and stop romanticizing things. I want a relationship with a man—a real man, not some fictional version who's all hearts and flowers. I won't let unrealistic and childish expectations sabotage a chance with this guy.

Gathering my composure, I step out of the bathroom, heading back to the kitchen to join Krew. "Do you need help with anything?"

"Grab two beers from the fridge. The pizza's almost done."

"Where's your glasses?"

"I don't need a glass. The bottle works just fine." Glasses?"

"I'm not legal." I pull up the sleeve of my hoodie.

Krew's head snaps up. "You're not eighteen?"

"I'm eighteen, but I'm not legal to drink."

"I don't care how old you are," Krew says coolly. "No one's going to be checking IDs here." He pulls the pizza out of the oven and sets the hot tray on the stovetop. "Now get the beers, and let's eat."

Four beers and a frozen pizza later, my head is feeling all kinds of fuzzy. Krew watches me from across the table. Struggling to maintain eye contact, I grapple with uncertainty about what to say or do next.

"I guess I should probably get going," I say awkwardly.

Krew takes a long pull from his bottle before replying, "I wasn't finished with you yet." He leans forward, resting his elbows on the table.

"Oh?" I ask, surprised.

"I want you in my bedroom." Slowly, I get to my feet. "Now." He follows close behind me as we enter his room. "Take your clothes off," he orders.

I turn to face him. My heart pounds and my palms are sweaty. I look at Krew's dark eyes and swallow hard. I don't know what to do.

"I said take off your clothes."

His gaze tracks the path of my hands as they reach for the hem of my shirt and slowly pull it over my head. I remove the rest of my clothes and stand naked before him. Krew looks me up and down. My cock is swollen and hard. Pre-cum beads on the tip, and I hope I don't embarrass myself and come too fast.

Krew removes his black biker jacket, tossing it casually onto the dresser. Following that, he peels off his white T-shirt. "Holy shit," I murmur.

Krew smirks.

I itch to reach out and run my hand along the well-defined muscles of his chest and stomach. To drag my tongue over his tattoos.

He kicks off his black leather boots and then lowers his pants. His cock is erect, and I swear, even bigger than it was earlier. My cock twitches in response to the incredible site standing in front of me.

"Do you like what you see?"

"Very much," I say and take a step toward him. I can't help myself. I reach out to touch him, but he catches my wrist.

"Turn around. I want you on your hands and knees." I walk to the bed and do as he instructs. "Spread your legs." I spread them wide apart and look over my shoulder. "You like being told what to do, don't you?" he asks as he strokes his cock.

"Yes."

"As long as you're in my bed, I'm in charge, and you'll call me master."

His demanding tone intensifies my arousal even further. "Yes, master."

"That's a good boy." He smacks my ass.

"Put your head down and spread your ass wide open for me."

I lower my head onto the bed and spread my cheeks wide. Krew drags his finger around my entrance. "I'm going to fuck this tight hole." His breathing becomes heavier as he leans over my back. His mouth is close to my ear. "I'm going to fuck you hard and make you beg for me to come inside you."

"Please be gentle," I say quietly.

"I don't do gentle, Leo." He spits on his hand and rubs it on his cock. Positioning himself behind me, he pushes his thick cock into my ass. Red searing pain blurs my vision. I bite down on my lip to keep from crying out as every muscle in my body tenses.

"You're resisting," he says with a strained tone as he continues to force my body to take him. "Let me in." I close my eyes and try to relax. "That's it," he says as he pushes in deeper. My body burns as it stretches to accommodate him. "I want you to beg me to fuck you."

"Please, fuck me," I say.

His hand makes contact with my ass. "What did I tell you?"

"Please fuck me, master, I beg.

Krew grabs my hips and pushes the rest of the way in. His dick is so big it feels as though I'm being split open, and I cry out.

"You like my cock in your ass, don't you?"

It hurts, but at the same time, it feels so good. "Yes," I say quietly.

He strikes me painfully hard. "Yes, what?"

"Yes, master."

"Say it," he demands as he pulls almost all the way out.

"I like your cock in my ass, master."

He slams into me. "That's a good boy." Krew grabs my hair, pulling my head back. "Do you want to come too?" I nod. "Beg."

"Please, master." My tone is desperate. "Please, can I come too?""

He reaches around and grabs my balls. "Come for me, boy."

That small amount of contact is all I need. "Oh my God," I scream as my cock explodes. My body convulses as I shoot waves of cum onto the bed. I've never come so hard.

"Good boy," he whispers.

His grip on my hips tightens. Krew holds me in place as he pounds into me.

"You're mine, boy."

"Yes, master."

His thrusts become faster and harder.

"Do you like my dick in your ass?" I nod. "Tell me."

"I love your dick in my ass, master."

Krew growls as he slams into me over and over. He's getting close.

"Come in my ass."

His balls slap against me as he fucks me wildly. "Fuck," he roars as he pulls out and spurts cum all over my back. A moment later, the bed dips as he gets up, leaving me alone.

"I asked you to come inside me," I say, hating the needy tone in my voice.

"You didn't call me master," he says as he pulls his jeans up. "You won't make that mistake again, will you boy?"

"No, master." Between the alcohol and the sex, I'm exhausted and can't keep my eyes open.

"You're going to make a good little play toy," he says and walks out of the room, leaving me alone.

Anthony

Adjusting to a new normal is a slow but ongoing process. New York City has forever changed since September 11th. Yet, each sunrise, each new day bears the promise of healing and the growth of newfound resilience.

With my coffee in hand, I walk the final few blocks to what will be my restaurant. Al and his crew have made significant progress over the past several weeks, and he needs me to sign off on a few things. Margot, my childhood friend and interior designer, will also be there. When I open the door, I'm hit with a gust of warm air, a nice change from the ice-cold winter air outside.

"Tony," Margot says coming over. "It's good to see you."

"You too." I kiss her cheek.

"Al and his team have been hard at work." She motions around the room. "What do you think?"

Stepping back to take it all in, I see the changes around me. New walls have been raised in once-empty areas. A crew of men is hard at work placing the quartz countertop, a focal point in the room. Its blues, greens, and white veining resemble the whitecaps on the sea.

"It's all falling into place." A familiar ache grips my chest as I realize Kameron should be here. This wasn't solely my dream. It was ours—a shared vision.

"Anthony?" Margot uses my full name. Something she only ever does when she's frustrated.

"I'm sorry. Can you repeat that?"

"I was saying before we delve into design decisions, Al needs your approval for the installation of the French Doors."

"I didn't know they were done."

The pocket doors in the archway open. "We're about a week ahead of schedule," Al informs as he walks into the room.

"I'm truly impressed with everything." I shake his hand, conveying my admiration. "The progress you've made since my last visit is nothing short of remarkable."

With a pleased nod, he replies, "I'm happy you like it."

Peeking over his shoulder into the back room, my eyes land on the doors. Leading the duo through the future main dining area, we step into the private back room. "They're breathtaking," I express as I swing open the oak doors to gauge the atmosphere. Glancing back at Margot, I acknowledge, "Your suggestion for the solid glass panes was spot on. Once summer comes and the gardens are in full bloom, they'll provide a spectacular view."

"If you're good with the installation, I'll grab your signature and get out of your way." Al passes me an electronic tablet, and I sign the screen with my finger.

After bidding farewell to Al, Margot and I dive into the tasks at hand. After settling on ivory walls and mid-tone grey travertine tile for the floor, Margot pulls up the digital blueprints for the grand archway—the focal piece for the restaurant. The wall around it will become a living wall with ivy growing and trailing along a manufactured branch.

"The lanterns suspended from the branches will create a warm and inviting ambiance," she describes. "What do you think?"

"It's absolutely breathtaking," I reply, leaning back. "I can't believe that my dream of owning a restaurant is finally materializing after all this time."

"It's the only thing you ever talked about as kids," she laughs softly.

Margot and I shared the same neighborhood growing up—she was the girl next door. Fostering my love for cooking and my entrepreneurial aspirations, my parents set up a play restaurant on the lower level of our house. On weekends, our friends would come over and be the diners. I'd whip up small snacks while Margot played the role of my waitress. "You were always such a good sport."

"You made it easy," she says, a warm smile gracing her lips. "Did you ever wonder what would happen if we got together?" Margot asks and places her delicate hand on my arm. For years, my parents had subtly hoped I'd date Margot, and that hope was one reason I chose to come out to them when I did. Fortunately, they were nothing but supportive. "It's not too late, Tony," she says softly. "I'm willing to share you with a man. I'd be happy just having a small piece of your heart."

"I'll always love you—as a friend. But you deserve more than to have a piece of someone's heart." Placing my hand over hers, I give it a tender squeeze. "There's a man out there ready to give you the moon and stars. He'll pick you above everyone else. And you deserve nothing less."

Margot rests her head on my shoulder. "Can't blame a girl for trying."

"You should come to the club. My friend Alex is single, and I think you'd hit it off."

"As if," she laughs. "The kink scene isn't my cup of tea." Motioning towards the samples we've selected, she asks, "Are you happy with what we've chosen?"

Contemplating the assembled mix of textures and colors, I confidently answer, "I think they'll work perfectly."

"I'll order everything tomorrow," she says as she closes her laptop. "Between the high-end décor and the five-star food, this will be New York's hottest restaurant."

Now it's my turn to laugh. "I think you're dreaming a little too big."

"What's that saying about dreaming big and reaching the stars?"

Once upon a time, I had big dreams for this place. Then, my world fell apart. Now, those dreams are overshadowed by tragedy. "Would you care to join me for a bite to eat before you go home?"

"I'd love that." She pulls her bag onto her shoulder and then links her arm with mine as we step out into the brisk evening air.

Piercing the evening sky, two beams of sapphire light stand tall. "I completely forgot they were illuminating the Tribute in Light tonight," I whisper, stirred by the view.

A heavy silence envelops Margot and me as we stand motionless for several minutes, each of us offering a silent tribute to the six-monthanniversary of the tragedy that shook the world.

It's just after eleven pm when Margot and I finish our dinner. The memorial lights have been extinguished, plunging the sky into darkness. With the late hour, the air has gotten significantly colder. I pull on my hat and wrap my scarf around my face to shield me from the wintery chill. After walking Margot to the subway station, I turn around to go back to the restaurant. Somehow, I forgot my phone there and need to grab it before going home.

Macdougal St. is an eclectic mix of shops and restaurants. During the day, it's a bustling street full of tourists and locals alike. At this hour, however, the street is eerily deserted, with businesses closed until dawn.

Turning the key to unlock the door, I step into the shadows

of my restaurant. Choosing a subdued ambiance, I illuminate only half the space. Even though I was here earlier, I can't resist the urge to linger and admire the extensive work that has transformed this place. Wandering through the main room, I imagine a backdrop of soft music accompanying diners relishing the delectable offerings before them.

The allure of the French Doors beckons me. Despite the bitter cold, I swing them open and step outside. Adding to the charm of this property is the expansive green space. Securing it was a stroke of luck. My vision for this space is to transform it into a flourishing garden, with one section designated for al fresco dining and the rest dedicated to cultivating an array of fresh ingredients.

A sharp, unexpected shattering of glass disrupts the quiet, and I go back inside to investigate the noise.

"We don't want any fucking terrorists in this neighborhood." Another of my front windows explodes as something is thrown through it. "Towel heads are not welcome. Go back where you came from," a male voice yells.

"What the hell?" I hurry toward the front of my restaurant.

"There's someone inside," one of them yells. "Let's get out of here."

Grabbing my phone off the table, I fumble with the screen to open my camera app as one of the people stops and yells, "Take your raghead and get the fuck out of our country." I take several pictures before they turn and run after their cohorts.

My attempt to vocalize something, anything, proves futile as my voice fails me. In their eyes, I'm one of *them*—the terrorists who changed our city, hell, our entire country on September 11th. Why? Is it because my skin isn't as white as theirs? Or because my hair and eyes are darker than they deem appropriate?

For the first time since the towers collapsed, stealing Kam from me, I feel soul-consuming hatred.

"Fuck," I shout as I turn and drive my fist through the glass door, shattering it just like the adjacent windows. Blood oozes from my knuckles, but I ignore it. Storming through the restaurant, I overturn the only table that's there.

Tears cascade down my cheeks, the agony of being labeled a terrorist and likened to the darkness that stole Kameron engulfing me. I stagger through the room, grappling to draw my next breath. A piercing pain slices through my chest, and I'm convinced I'm having a heart attack. Crossing the threshold into my office, I slump against the wall, embracing the thought of death—a welcome reunion with Kameron.

Anthony

"Tony," a familiar voice cuts through the black fog surrounding me. I push the hand off my shoulder, reluctant to leave the dream realm. In that world, Kameron and I exist together. When I open my eyes, Kameron will disappear, and I'll be alone again. "Tony. Wake up."

Grudgingly, my eyelids blink open and slowly begin to focus. "What are you doing here?"

"I got a call from the NYPD that they were looking for you," Owen explains. "They went to your apartment building, but you weren't there either. The super gave the police your emergency contact information."

"Why are they looking for me?" I rub my eyes.

"The guy who owns the business next door saw the mess when he went to open his shop this morning and called the police." He looks down at my hand, that's covered in dried blood. "What the hell happened here?"

I push up off the floor and get to my feet as I recount the events of last night. "They think I'm one of *them*," I yell and grab my chest as another pain slices through my chest.

"What's wrong?" Owen asks as he grabs my arm.

"Nothing." I attempt to take a step and nearly fall over as blackness creeps into my vision.

"Sit down." Owen helps me to my desk chair. "I'm calling an ambulance."

"I don't want an ambulance."

"Is this Mr. Genovese?" an NYPD officer steps into the doorway of my office.

Owen holds up a finger while he relays information to the 911 operator on the phone. "He's having chest pain and nearly lost consciousness." A pause. "Okay, thank you." He disconnects the call. "Sorry." He turns to face the officer. "I think he's having a heart attack. There's an ambulance on the way."

The officer approaches, stooping to my eye level. "Mr. Genovese, are you having trouble breathing?" he asks.

"Unfortunately, no," I mutter. "And call me Tony."

"Tony, I'm Officer Lucero," he says, standing. "Are you able to tell me anything that happened here?"

Owen steps between the police officer and me. "Do we really have to do this right now? Can't it wait until after he receives medical attention?"

"I'm fine," I interrupt Owen. "I was here last night to grab my phone when three men started yelling racial slurs and smashed my windows." I stop to catch my breath.

Officer Lucero nods sympathetically, responding, "Unfortunately, since the attack on the towers, we've seen an increase in hate crimes."

"I'm Italian, not Muslim!" I shout, the pain returning with such intensity that I find myself reaching for the chair.

"We're done here until after he sees a doctor," Owen insists. There's a flurry of activity outside of the office as two EMTs arrive on the scene.

Officer Lucero steps aside, allowing the EMTs to initiate their assessment. They bombard me with medical questions,

"We're going to do a quick EKG," the female EMT says as she puts stickers on my chest and hooks them up to some wires while simultaneously hooking me up to machines for blood pressure, oxygen, and heart rate measurements.

"This is all really unnecessary," I protest, rolling my eyes.

"That's okay if it is," she says, offering me a reassuring smile. "It gives us some extra practice."

After they're done with their initial assessment, they get me settled on a stretcher and load me into the back of an ambulance. Memories of Kameron's body being put into the back of a similar ambulance flood to the surface. My heart rate skyrockets, causing everyone to descend on me.

Once they're certain death is imminent, they allow Owen to climb in.

"You really don't have to come. I'm sure you have better things to do."

"There's nowhere else I need to be," Owen says as he sits on a bench off to the side.

With lights flashing and sirens wailing, the ambulance maneuvers through the city streets.

Anthony

My arrival at the ER was met with a line of doctors and nurses ready to save a man suspected of dying from a heart attack. Vials of blood were drawn, and I was hooked up to more machines. Once they determined I was stable, a physician's assistant cleaned up my bleeding hand. He told me I was lucky to only have minor cuts and scratches.

We've been here for hours. The constant beep from the monitor tracking the rhythm of my heart is starting to drive me crazy.

"Clearly, I'm fine. Can you get a nurse so I can sign myself out?" I ask, annoyed.

"No," Owen says without looking up from his phone. "We're waiting until you see a doctor."

We revert to tense silence, waiting for a physician. A knock on the door breaks the stillness.

"Hi. I'm Dr. Patel," the man in the white coat says as he approaches the bed. "I apologize for the long wait."

When I don't respond, Owen takes charge. "It's not a problem."

"I've reviewed your test results," he explains. "Everything looks okay."

"He didn't have a heart attack?" Owen asks, surprised.

"It doesn't appear that way. His cardiac enzymes, troponin, and CPK are within normal range." The doctor rattles off his medical jargon. "His EKG showed tachycardia, but no ST elevations, indicating what Mr. Genovese experienced was most likely stress related." He takes his stethoscope from around his neck. "Do you mind if I do a quick exam?"

"If it gets me out of here sooner, go right ahead."

"Have you been experiencing any other symptoms?" Dr. Patel asks.

"Sometimes my heart feels like it's beating too fast. But it goes away quickly." I shrug.

"How long has this been going on?" He types something into his laptop.

"I don't know," I respond, holding onto the unspoken truth that it's happened since a part of my heart died.

Leaning against the counter opposite my bed, the doctor explains, "I suspect you may have had an anxiety attack."

"I knew I didn't need to come to the hospital." I shoot Owen an annoyed glare.

"The symptoms often mimic those of a heart attack. It's a good thing you decided to come in for a check-up," he adds quickly. "Are you still experiencing shortness of breath or chest pain?"

I hesitate, looking between Owen and the doctor, who are both watching me expectantly. "A bit."

"There's a medication we often prescribe for anxiety. Would you be open to trying it to see if it helps?"

"If I try it, how much longer do I need to stay?"

"Once you take it, you should start to feel better in fifteen to twenty minutes," he says patiently. "Then, as long as you're okay, I'll get your discharge papers and let you go home."

"Fine." I rest my head back and look at the ceiling.

"I'll go put the order in. A nurse will bring it to you shortly," the doctor states as he walks toward the door.

"Thanks, doctor," Owen says appreciatively.

When the door clicks closed, I sit up and say, "I told you there was nothing wrong with me."

"That's not exactly what the doctor said," Owen states.

"Whatever." I know my annoyance with him is misplaced, but I can't help myself.

The room feels saturated with an unspoken heaviness, an all-encompassing force that seeps into every nook and cranny. Neither of us utters a word, and right now, silence is a blessing. Conversation is the last thing on my mind.

The nurse takes an agonizingly long time to deliver the medication. The nurse finally arrives with the medication, but her explanation becomes background noise. I tune her out, watching her lips move without absorbing any of the words.

"You might get a little drowsy," she explains after I dissolve the little white pill under my tongue. "Don't hesitate to use your call button if you need anything."

"Can you take this out?" I point to the IV in my arm.

"Not yet," she says apologetically. "I'll be back to check on you in a little bit."

With spread legs, Owen leans forward, burying his head in his hands. I mirror his action, dropping my head back and closing my eyes. I never take pills, so I feel the effects quickly.

"Tony," Owen says, looking up at me. "I think you need to talk to someone."

"What?"

"About Kam's death." He sits up straight. "I don't think you've dealt with the loss."

"I'm fine."

"That's what I mean. Your concern is always focused on being strong for everyone else. So much so that I don't think you've allowed yourself to grieve your loss. And this, today, brought it all to a head." I open my mouth to speak, but he shakes his head. "You didn't have a heart attack—this time. But if you don't deal with everything simmering below the surface, you might not be so lucky next time."

Though I recognize the truth in his words, admitting it feels like an admission of defeat. "I've tried so hard," my voice falters, catching on the lump in my throat. "I thought I was doing okay. But they compared me to the terrorists. The ones whose actions led to Kam's death. I snapped." I meet Owen's gaze. "At that moment, I didn't care if I lived or died. Actually." I correct myself. "That's not true. I welcomed death. How could they do that?" Tears stream down my cheeks. "Why would anyone say something so hurtful?"

"There's no excuse for what they said and did." Owen gets to his feet and sits on the edge of my bed. "They'll get what's coming to them. But right now, I'm more concerned about you. Are you ready to let someone help you heal?"

It's as though a dam has burst, and I find myself unable to contain the torrent of emotions. A feeble nod escapes me just before I feel Owen's strong arms enveloping me in a supportive embrace.

"I'm sorry to interrupt," the nurse steps into the room. "I can come back."

"You good?" Owen asks quietly.

"Yeah." I wipe my face with the back of my hands. "Come in."

She looks between us curiously as Owen returns to his seat. "I was just checking to see how you're feeling."

"Much better," I convey with a small, appreciative smile.

"Good." She hesitates. "There are two NYPD officers in the hall. They said they need to speak with you."

"I told them they were going to need to wait," Owen says, getting to his feet. "I'll get rid of them."

"It's okay," I say, stopping him. "Tell them to come in so I can give my statement."

"Are you sure?" he asks.

"The sooner I tell them what happened, the sooner they can find out who did this."

"I'll let them know they can come in," the nurse says.

I spend the next half hour giving my statement to Officer Lucero and his partner, including giving him the pictures from my cell phone.

"Thank you for your cooperation, Tony," he says as he finishes writing in his notebook. "We'll do everything to be sure these people are brought to justice."

Leopold

"I HAVE TO GO OUT," KREW YELLS INTO THE BEDROOM where I'm getting dressed. "Make sure this kitchen is cleaned up before I get back."

"I will," I call as I hear the door slam.

I'm in the middle of doing the dishes when my phone rings. Glancing at the caller ID, I see it's Ramiro. I've been dodging his calls for the past week, but I'm unsure what to say. I know I can't avoid him forever. Now seems as good a time as any. "Hello?"

"I've been trying to get in touch with you for days," Ramiro says when the call connects.

"I'm sorry about that. I've been a little busy." I wipe my hands on the dish rag.

"You haven't been back to the center. Where are you?" he asks, concern evident in his voice. "I've been staying with a friend."

"Frank called earlier," Ramiro informs me. "He said you've missed three of your shifts. That's not like you. What's going on?"

"Um." I sink onto the couch. "My friend wasn't feeling well, and I've been taking care of them."

"Try again, Leo." Ramiro isn't convinced. "I know when I'm being lied to."

There's a long pause while I try to come up with something. Fumbling with my words, I mutter. "I'll be at work tomorrow."

"I hate to do this, Leo, but you'll need to come pick up your things."

"What?"

"We discussed the rules when you moved in," he clarifies, emphasizing the importance. "If you're gone for longer than forty-eight hours without prior approval, you automatically forfeit your room at Safe Haven."

"I'm sorry," I say quickly as panic surges through me. "I'll be back tonight."

"I wish I could bend the rules for you, I really do, but there's a mandatory six-month wait period before you'll be eligible for a room again."

"Shit," I mumble.

"When you come to get your things, I'll give you a list of local shelters," Ramiro offers, compassion in his voice.

"Thanks."

We disconnect the call, and after I take a few seconds to calm down, I get back to the dishes. Krew and I haven't talked about my living arrangements. I've been staying at his apartment since the night we met. He seems to enjoy having me in his bed, but we haven't broached the topic of how long I'll be staying.

As I clean up the house, I rehearse how I'll bring up the subject when Krew gets home. The last thing I want is to stumble over my words like a bumbling fool. But how do you ask a guy you met just a week ago if there's potential for more than a passing fling?

I'm still working out the correct phrasing when I hear the apartment door open and Krew's heavy footsteps echo in the other room. "Where are you?"

"Right here." I step out of the bedroom. "I was just making the bed."

"The place looks good. I'll have to give you a reward later," he says, lowering his voice in that sexy way that makes my stomach get butterflies. Krew isn't the romantic, touchy-feely, kinda man I always imagined falling for, but not much in life has turned out the way I'd hoped. But what he lacks in affection, he makes up for in so many other ways.

"I have to go back out," he says as he pulls his T-shirt over his head and tosses it onto the bedroom floor. Opening a drawer, he grabs a clean black shirt and walks out of the room.

"Do you have to go right now?" I ask, following him.

"Why? Do you have plans I don't know about?" he asks, slightly annoyed.

"Kind of." I exhale slowly. "There's something I need to talk to you about."

Krew leans against the edge of the kitchen counter and crosses his arms over his chest. "Go on."

Everything I'd practiced seems to have vanished. "I don't have an actual apartment. The place I live." I stumble over my words. "It's called Safe Haven. It's a program—" I realize he's starting to tune me out, so I fast forward some. "I'm not supposed to be gone for more than 48 hours without checking in with them. I didn't do that, and I lost my room. They called while you were out and told me I have to pick up my things." I search Krew's face, but he doesn't give away his thoughts. "This past week has been great, but I don't want you to feel like you have to let me move in."

"Put your shoes on so we can go grab your shit." He pushes off the counter and grabs his black leather jacket.

"I can stay here?" I ask, surprised.

"That depends," he says with a seductive smile. I don't have time to contemplate what he means before he points. "Get on your knees."

I lower to the floor and open my mouth as he pulls out his hard cock. Without warning, he grabs a handful of hair as he thrusts deep. I've become adept at relaxing my throat, a skill acquired through intensive practice over the last few days. My dick strains against my zipper, but I know the rules and don't touch myself. Any pleasure I get comes only with Krew's expressed consent.

He fucks my face hard and fast before letting out a loud groan as he comes down my throat. After I lick him clean, he tucks himself into his pants.

"Let's go." He walks toward the door, and I scramble to get to my feet. "We need to be back before my friends get here."

"Are you coming in?" I ask when we get to the building.

Krew lights a cigarette. "I'll wait out here. Don't be long."

When I get inside, I stop at reception and wait to be let into the back offices. Ramiro's sitting behind his desk, taking a phone call. He motions for me to come in. Quietly, I sit and wring my hands in my lap while I wait for him to finish his call.

"It's good to see you," he says when he hangs up.

"You too." I look around the room. "Do you have my things? I'm kind of in a hurry."

"I'll get them in a minute. There're a few papers you need to sign first."

"Okay."

"This one outlines the reasons why you—" He stops talking when I grab a pen and scribble my name. "You shouldn't sign anything before you know what it is."

"Like I said, I don't have much time. Krew's waiting for me."

"Krew? As in Krew Ramos?"

"Yeah, I guess." I give a casual shrug, a touch of embarrassment creeping in. His last name wasn't on my mind the night we crossed paths, and I haven't thought to inquire about it since then.

"Please tell me you're not mixed up with him." There's a pleading tone in Ramiro's voice. "He's not a good guy."

"He treats me well," I argue.

"Listen to me, Leo." Ramiro leans forward, resting his elbows on his desk. "There's only one Krew around here, and he's not someone you should be hanging around with."

"I'm certain you're talking about the wrong person." I stand up. "Like I said, I'm in a hurry."

"There's a six-month waiting period before you can reapply for a room with Safe Haven." Ramiro slides a packet of papers across his desk. "Here's a list of shelters. Please call one of them and find somewhere to stay."

"Can I get my things?" I ask impatiently. "I really need to go."

Ramiro pushes to his feet and walks to his office closet. He reaches in and grabs a black duffle bag. Turning back to me, he says, "Please promise me you won't go home with him. I don't want to see you get hurt."

"I assure you everything's good." I reach out and take my bag. "Thanks again for everything." I ignore Ramiro's warning and walk away.

When I get back outside, Krew is pacing while talking on the phone. "He's here now. We're on our way." He disconnects his call and slides the phone into his front pocket. "It took you long enough."

"Leo, wait," Ramiro's urgent voice reaches me as he hurries through the glass doors to catch up. "It breaks every rule, and I could lose my job for doing this. Come and stay at my place. Just don't go with him." Time seems to freeze as I glance between the two men.

"Are you fucking this loser, too?" Krew asks, grabbing my arm.

"Back off, Krew," Ramiro warns.

"Or what?"

"I'm only with you," I say, putting my hand on Krew's chest, hoping to back him down. "I've told you that."

Krew directs his gaze over my shoulder toward Ramiro. The stark differences between them are impossible to miss. Krew's jet-black hair falls untamed, accentuated by the worn black leather jacket that hugs his broad shoulders. His hours at the gym are evident, even if the hottest part of him—his tattooed back—is currently concealed.

On the flip side, there's Ramiro. Considerably shorter than Krew, his brown hair is always meticulously groomed. Clad in the usual khaki pants and a polo shirt, he exudes the aura of the stereotypical preppy guy—the good guy everyone would advise me to listen to. Instead, I find myself clinging to Krew.

"Tell him who you belong to," Krew whispers so only I can hear.

I turn to face Ramiro. "I'm with Krew. I'm his now," I say, keeping my voice steady.

"You have my number," Ramiro says, his shoulders falling in defeat. "Call me anytime."

"Fuck off, Vega." Krew takes my hand. "Let's go."

"My offer's always open," Ramiro calls after us.

Leopold

Krew was quiet on the way home. He spent most of it texting back and forth with someone. It isn't until we get home that I find the courage to ask, "Is everything okay?"

"No." He slides his phone into the pocket of his jeans. "I have to go out for a while."

"Are you going to be late?" I hate that I sound so needy.

Krew pins me with his stare. "You move in, and now I have a curfew?"

"Of course not," I say quickly. "It's just if you're going to be late, I might be asleep already."

"Why?"

"I have to work in the morning."

"You didn't tell me you had a job."

"It hasn't come up in conversation." I shrug. "I work part-time at North Park Bodega."

"I know the place." Krew grabs the keys to his motorcycle. "Blow off work tomorrow."

"If I *blow off* work again, I'll lose my job."

"That's fine with me," he says as he heads for the door.

"I need my job." I follow him, hoping to get him to see reason. "I can't go without money."

Krew turns to face me. "You live in my house now, and I don't want you working for them." I drop my head and sigh. "Don't you trust me to take care of you?" he asks, lifting my chin with his finger.

Do I trust him? I've only known him for a short time, but he's been good to me, and now he's extended an invitation to live with him. That must mean he feels something more. Right?

If that's true, why do Ramiro's warnings echo in the recesses of my mind? The initial belief that Ramiro was referring to someone else was shattered when they confronted each other. It's evident—they not only recognized each other but also shared a mutual dislike. That shouldn't surprise me. Ramiro tends to be more conservative with his choice of associates.

Krew watches me closely, waiting for my answer.

"Yes," I respond, silently wrestling with the doubts swirling within me, hoping they don't overshadow my words. "I trust you."

"Good. Text them and quit."

"But—"

"If it means that much to you," Krew drawls. "You can work for me."

"I'd really appreciate that."

"Good." He leans in and kisses me. "We'll talk more about it tomorrow."

After Krew leaves, I settle on the sofa next to my black duffel. All of my worldly possessions fit into this one bag, a thought that weighs heavily on me. Yet, in the same breath, I find a glimmer of hope. I'm no longer confined to a nondescript shelter room—a castaway from society. Now, I have an apartment with my boyfriend. It's a step up.

Even though I'm uneasy about leaving my job and relying on Krew, he did mention discussing how I could earn a living working for him. I'm unsure about his line of work, but hopefully, it's something I'll be good at.

With trembling hands, I reach for my cell and open a new text.

Leo: Do you have a minute?

Frank: I have a line right now. I'll check the messages when I can.

I take my time to decide what to say next.

Leo: Unfortunately, I won't be able to continue working. I'm grateful for the opportunity, but my circumstances have changed.

Pressing send, I wait for a reply. When none arrives, I grab my bag and head to the bedroom to organize my belongings. Krew has graciously allowed me to use his clothes this past week, but with him being taller and more solidly built, they don't fit quite right. It'll be nice to have my own clothes to wear.

Compared to Krew, I don't have much. I make space in one of his drawers for my pants and hang my handful of T-shirts in the closet. Since there's no toothbrush holder, I place mine next to his on the bathroom sink.

Returning to the living room, I check my phone, but there's still no response. With the house in order, there's nothing to do until Krew gets home. I switch on the television, hoping to find something to watch. While flipping through the channels, my phone dings.

Frank: I don't understand what's going on. When I hired you, we discussed that you'd give notice if you were going to leave your job. You've been a no-show three shifts in a row, and now you just up and quit?

I hate doing this to Frank. He hired me based on Ramiro's recommendation. Because of this, I'll stain not only Ramiro's word but also my own name. But I'm helpless to stop myself because of my desperation to please Krew.

It's in the way he gazes at me, his eyes filled with lust, just before he fills me. The way his hand tangles in my hair or wraps around my throat moments before he closes his eyes and releases inside me—it's a potent mix, one I crave. The empowerment I feel, knowing it's my body providing him pleasure, is intoxicating.

I've wanted a man to look at me the way Krew does for so long, I'm not willing to give it up.

Leo: Like I said, things have changed for me. I no longer live at the shelter, and my commute would be too long.

Frank: I was speaking with Ramiro earlier today. He didn't tell me you left the program.

I don't like being dishonest, but I feel like there's no other choice.

Leo: I asked him not to say anything.

Frank: This feels very out of character. Like there's more to this story.

Krew's very private, and knowing he doesn't like Frank means I must be extra cautious about what I say.

Leo: The truth is, I met someone. I hadn't said anything to Ramiro about it until earlier today. We decided to move in together, and he lives on the other side of the city. Unfortunately, working for you isn't going to be practical.

Frank: At the risk of sounding too much like your parents, I think you're moving too fast.

Leo: I appreciate your concern.

Frank: You understand because you didn't keep your end of the agreement up to give notice before quitting, I won't be able to provide you with a reference for your next job.

Leo: I understand. I'm sorry it had to be this way.

Frank: Good luck, Leo.

Dropping the phone into my lap, I let my head fall back onto the sofa. Burning bridges has never been my style—it's not a wise move. However, even in the short time we've been together, I have to trust that Krew cares about me as much as I've grown to care about him. People like Frank, observing from the outside, might think I'm moving too fast, but when you realize you're falling in love, there's no reason to wait.

For the first time in my life, I'm actually looking forward to the future.

Anthony

I CAUTIOUSLY ENTER THE STREAM OF LIFE CHURCH through its side door, uncertain about what awaits me inside. Their online bulletin board ad painted a picture of a dynamic and inclusive community that embraces individuals from diverse backgrounds. Curiosity gets the better of me, prompting me to give it a shot.

After the intervention from Owen and experiencing a miniature emotional breakdown, I've come to the realization that maybe I need to address my emotions. Kameron's absence is a harsh reality—I can no longer avoid the truth that he won't be coming back. The dreams we once shared for our future now linger as bittersweet memories. For the past six months, I've been navigating life without a clear sense of purpose.

Owen's advice rings true. I can't continue in this state of emotional limbo. It's time to lay Kameron and our shared dreams to rest and embark on a journey to discover a new path in life.

"Welcome to Loving Arms," a petite brunette woman with an edgy undercut says. "I'm Pastor Andrea." Her appearance defies the traditional pastor stereotype, instantly putting my mind at ease."I'm Tony," I introduce myself, shaking her hand. "Pleasure to meet you."

"We're just about to get started. Grab a coffee and a seat." She smiles warmly.

A large metal coffee maker, reminiscent of the one my parents used for holiday parties, sits on a rectangular folding table. I grab a Styrofoam cup and fill it almost to the brim, leaving no room for cream. Taking a cautious sip, I navigate my way to find a seat.

The room is filled with white plastic folding chairs arranged in a spacious circle, with only two left unoccupied.

"Hi," the woman in the adjacent seat greets me.

"Hi," I reply, reciprocating the friendly gesture as we settle into the circle.

"Good evening," Pastor Andrea gathers the group. "It's wonderful to see everyone here tonight. First, let me apologize—I ran out of nametags and forgot to order more." She chuckles. "So, we're going to do this the old-fashioned way. We'll go around the circle, say our names, and if you're comfortable, share a bit about why you're here. It'll help facilitate our conversations and hopefully support you in your grieving process."

I listen attentively as each person makes their introductions. Some keep it concise, while others speak openly. I learn that the woman seated beside me goes by the name Jennifer. Her loss also occurred on September 11th, and it becomes evident that she's a regular attendee.

When it's my turn, I muster the strength to speak. "Hi, my name's Tony," I begin. "My partner, Kameron, was a Fire Chief in the FDNY. He was in the North Tower when it collapsed." Emotions overpower me, and my voice falters.

"We're glad to have you with us," Pastor Andrea says warmly.

"Now that we're all friends, we can move on," Kelly chimes in with a grin, "We often discuss the process of grieving and what to expect. Tonight, I'd like to explore something a little different. As you know, no two individuals experience grief exactly the same way." She pauses for a sip of her coffee. "Even though there are steps we can expect to move through in processing our loss, unexpected things often occur. Would anyone be willing to share something they've found surprising, frustrating—anything other than," Kelly air quotes, "by the book?"

Several people shift nervously in their seats before Jennifer slowly raises her hand. "I'd like to share something."

Kelly motions with her hand. "The group is all yours."

"Most of you are aware that my three-year-old has been struggling since Jeff passed." Several heads nod. "Last week was Jeff's birthday. I didn't know what to do—should I let it pass quietly or honor him? Anna's therapist suggested we go ahead and have his favorite birthday dinner. We also decided to release balloons to Daddy in heaven," she says, shifting nervously in her seat. "It was a hard day. The girls were fighting all day. Anna was super clingy. Dinner ended up burning. It was a disaster. I was so mad at Jeff. He was supposed to be here raising the girls with me. I wasn't supposed to be alone." She looks up, her brown eyes glistening with tears.

"I'd given up and ordered takeout. When I sat on the couch, Chloe, my eighteen-month-old, started pulling at my leg. I tried to pick her up, but she wriggled out of my hold, telling me no. I was at my breaking point, but then she started pointing toward the kitchen, yelling *Daddy.* She was smiling and giggling. I know you'll all think I'm crazy, but I could feel him." Chills run down my body. "Even though I didn't see him, it helped me feel less alone. Reminded me that he's still here watching over me and the girls."

"That's beautiful," Kelly says, swiping at her eyes. "It's been said that those we love never really leave. They walk beside us every day."

"I'm a believer now," Jennifer says, laughing softly.

As the meeting progresses, a few group members share their unexpected experiences—some positive, others negative—each falling outside the realm of what's anticipated.

Pastor Andrea brings the official part of the meeting to a close. Some members hurriedly exit, while others linger, conversing in smaller groups. I dispose of my cup, check my phone for missed messages, and casually make my way toward the exit.

"The first few meetings can be overwhelming," Pastor Andrea notes as I approach the door. "But I hope you'll join us again."

"Yes, I plan to," I say, expressing my commitment.

"I'm glad to hear that," she says with a smile, offering me her card. "If you need anything during the week, don't hesitate to reach out."

Despite the cold, I choose to walk instead of taking the subway, allowing myself time for quiet reflection on tonight's group session. Initially, I went into it with the belief that I didn't truly need to be there, attributing my panic attack solely to the stress of the hate crime. However, as I sat there listening to others share their stories of loss, a profound realization struck me. I've never allowed myself to truly feel anything after Kameron's death.

Subconsciously, I've been avoiding the harsh reality, unwilling to accept the permanence of Kam's absence. I've been living in a state of denial, pretending he's away for work as he's done in the past. Like when he traveled to battle wildfires in California last year, spending weeks away. Despite the memorial service we had, I've never embraced the fact that he's really gone. Never allowed myself to feel the profound loss and grieve for the man I loved. Tonight's support group was a stark wake-up call. I've lost someone I love, and Kameron is truly gone—he's not coming back.

When I finally get home, I'm physically and mentally exhausted. I look out the floor-to-ceiling windows in my kitchen. Eight months later, the bright lights still shine at Ground Zero as work continues around the clock clearing the area. Construction workers and firefighters have painstakingly been clearing through the debris, hoping to find anything that'll give closure to the families whose loved ones have not been recovered. That hope dwindles a little more with each day that passes.

I still volunteer at the site a few times a month. The day after the attacks, we hastily organized a makeshift restaurant to provide sustenance for the weary rescue workers. Our operations have since moved to Trinity Church, located just across the street. Astonishingly, the building remained untouched and now serves as a twenty-four-seven place of respite.

Volunteers and emergency personnel put in days of relentless work without going home. Trinity becomes their refuge, providing not only a place to tend to their physical needs—offering showers, meals, and rest—but also a sanctuary for emotional and spiritual comfort amidst the challenging work they undertake.

Too tired to cook, I prepare a quick sandwich before showering and settling into bed. Tomorrow, I'll be at my restaurant, overseeing the installation of new windows and the sign I ordered. Once completed, there should be no doubt that I'm opening an Italian eatery with no connection to the terrorists.

Anthony

With many trades scheduled at the restaurant today and the kitchen still unusable, I make a stop at a local deli to pick up lunch meat and buns for everyone. A well-fed crew is a happy and productive crew. Although I'm just picking up a pre-order, there's a line. While waiting my turn, I check my email and find the confirmation for the class I signed up for at the local community center that starts later this afternoon.

I've always been the creative type. Back in high school, many years ago, I took art classes. During culinary school, I channeled my creativity into the plates I crafted. It wasn't until I met Kam and used his body as my canvas that I felt truly fulfilled. Now, with that outlet gone, a part of me feels empty.

I'm not ready to play with another sub. I don't know if I'll ever be ready. For now, I'm opting for a canvas and easel. Who knows, maybe I'll be the next Bob Ross. The notion prompts a spontaneous laugh, drawing curious glances from those around me. I quickly look down at my phone, pretending I'm watching a video and not laughing at my internal monologue.

When I get to my restaurant, the wood barricading the spaces where windows were missing has been taken down. One side has a newly installed window, and workers are currently getting the other side ready for replacement.

"Hello, Mr. Genovese," Abe, the foreman, says when he sees me. "What do you think?"

"It looks great." I inspect the side that's completed. "This has the force resistance glazing, right?"

"It does." He knocks on the glass. "Nothing is getting through these."

"Good." I nod. "I brought food for everyone. How about you all come in to eat?"

"That would be terrific." Abe turns to his workers. "You heard the man. It's lunchtime."

"Once the kitchen is finished, I'll invite everyone for a proper meal," I say as we enter the building. Setting the tray on the bar, I grab the paper plates and napkins I keep here for our working lunches. "There's bottled water in there," I point to the mini fridge on the bar.

While the men enjoy their meal, I head to the back of the restaurant, where the drywallers are on stilts mudding the tops of the walls. There's been significant progress since my last visit. I snap a few pictures and send them to Margot to keep her in the loop.

While waiting for the sign company to arrive, I sit down and pull out my sketch pad to work on the design for the back garden.

On the right side, accessible through the back door of the kitchen, a vegetable and herb garden will be surrounded by a privacy fence. *Italiano Desiderio's* appeal will include fresh, hand-made food. I plan to grow as many ingredients as possible, supplemented by sourcing from some of the best markets in Chelsea.

Outside the French doors will be a flower garden. Currently, the space features several mature trees. I plan to add a few more evergreens for year-round beauty. In spring, landscapers will plant this area with lush flowers that will bloom throughout the summer and into the fall.

There's another parcel of land for sale behind my current property that I'm in the process of purchasing. The plan for that space is to create an exclusive outdoor wedding venue—a dream Kam and I shared for our wedding if gay marriage ever became legalized. Since his death, I've struggled with whether I should continue with purchasing the space or if I should give up on it. Despite the heavy emotional weight, I've decided to continue pursuing the property.

As I sketch out plans for the flagstone path with deep purple creeping thyme growing between the stones, I envision the sides adorned with layers of pure white flowers that, under the moonlight, will appear to glow. At the end of the path, tall, wrought iron gates will open to an intimate venue area.

My concentration is interrupted when squeaky brakes outside catch my attention. I look up and see a bright yellow box truck with *Signs-R-Us* painted on the side. My heart picks up a beat as I stand and go outside to meet the installation crew. They inform me it'll take a few hours to get the sign in place. With the window crew finished, the sign installers can get right to work.

Not wanting to be in their way, I return inside and keep busy cleaning up the leftovers from lunch before sitting back down with my sketches. Just as I'm getting back into my creative stride, my phone rings. The name on the caller ID makes my pulse spike. Considering whether to send the call to voicemail, I decide at the last second to swipe the green button and answer.

"Hello?"

A familiar voice asks, "May I speak to Mr. Genovese?"

"This is him."

"It's Officer Lucero. I hope I didn't catch you at a bad time."

Is there ever a good time for the NYPD to call?

"No, you didn't," I reply. "How can I help you, Officer?"

"There's been a development in your case," he shares with me. "All three individuals linked to the incident at your restaurant have been apprehended."

My breath catches, and I quietly respond, "Oh."

"The trio is currently in police custody," he discloses, delivering the awaited news. "They face multiple charges, including criminal mischief and terroristic threats."

"What happens from here?"

"They're being held for arraignment. Two of the men have prior records. One was wanted on an outstanding warrant," he explains. "The third is a minor who already has quite an impressive record. Because of that, the district attorney is pushing for them to be held without bail."

"Is that something that can happen?" Shaken by the report, I close my sketchpad.

"Yes," Officer Lucero states matter-of-factly. "You'll probably be called to testify."

I slide my things into my brown leather messenger back. "Do I need a lawyer or something?"

"No," he chuckles and tries to cover it up with a cough. "The district attorney will be working on your behalf."

"Is there anything else I need to be aware of at this point?"

"Once a trial date is set, the DA's office will be in touch," Officer Lucero explains. "In the meantime, you have my number if you have any questions."

After we hang up, I take a few minutes to gather my thoughts. I really didn't think any arrests would be made. All I was able to give the officer was a blurry photo, not even a description. It wasn't until after everything happened that I had a discrete, high-quality security camera system put in place inside and outside the restaurant.

I've waited as long as I can to see the sign installed. However, the ticking clock reminds me of my impending art class. Stepping outside, I navigate carefully under the temporary scaffolding and shift my gaze upward. The sign, still being secured, proudly takes its place in the designated spot.

The hand-painted design exudes elegance with a touch of minimalism. *Italiano Desiderio* graces the façade in dark charcoal lettering. Below it, the phrase *Entri Come Amini, Vada Come Famiglia* extends a warm invitation. At night, soft backlighting will highlight the graceful script.

Witnessing my restaurant name on the building adds a tangible reality to my venture. However, the circumstances leading to this prompt installation tempers my excitement. Initially, I planned to unveil the sign once the interior was complete. Yet, in the aftermath of the hateful act that transpired here, I felt compelled to assert my identity and showcase the business so no one would be able to confuse me or my establishment again.

Leopold

Krew and I have been living together for almost a month now. Things between us are good. Actually, they're better than good. He's a sexy, alpha man who likes to take charge in and out of the bedroom. After living in such a restrictive environment at Walking in the Light, I didn't think I'd want to be in a relationship where I handed that much power to someone else, but surprisingly, this feels so right.

We've fallen into a comfortable rhythm, and despite enjoying my new domestic role, I still want to earn my own money. I'm not entirely comfortable with our current arrangement, where he covers all the expenses. Whenever I bring it up, Krew insists caring for me brings him joy. Then, the conversation is put to rest by him fucking me senseless.

Despite thoroughly enjoying every second with Krew, I've made up my mind to have a serious discussion with him when he returns home today. I need him to understand how important it is for me to have a job and earn a paycheck. My brief stint working for Frank left me with a deep sense of pride each time I received my wages—a sentiment I genuinely miss.

My phone is in my hand, and I'm scrolling down job listings when Krew gets home.

"We're having company tonight," he says in lieu of hello.

"Who's coming over?" I ask excitedly, setting my phone down.

"Some friends."

"Are they coming for dinner?"

"I'm sure we'll eat." He glances at me. "Call that Chinese restaurant and order a bunch of stuff." He opens his wallet and hands me a credit card. "I'm going to shower."

"Can we talk first?"

"About what?" he asks, his tone carries frustration.

"About my having a job."

"I thought we went over this already," he says as he kicks off his shoes.

"We did, sort of." I shrug. "You said we'd talk about me working for you, but we haven't actually—"

"Have I not been caring for you and ensuring you have everything you need?"

"Yes, but it's not the same as me paying my own way."

"Fine," he says as he walks down the hall toward his bedroom. "Order the food and make sure there's cold beer in the fridge." He slams his bedroom door shut, ending the conversation.

I drop my head on the couch. Upsetting him wasn't my intention. I guess it's all part of learning how to communicate with each other better—something I'm clearly not good at. The last thing I wanted to do was sound ungrateful for his generosity. Hopefully, he'll see reason when he thinks about it for a few minutes.

Krew's showers are usually pretty quick, so I don't waste any more time before calling the restaurant to order takeout. I'm cleaning off the cluttered counter when Krew returns to the kitchen. His dark hair hangs wet, and a few droplets of water drip onto his naked chest.

"Wow," I say and lick my lower lip.

"Is the food ordered?" he asks, ignoring me.

"It is. I don't know how many people are coming, so I ordered a lot."

"Two."

"Another couple?"

"Something like that," he says, not looking up from whoever he's texting.

"I'm sorry for upsetting you." I walk over to him and rub his shoulders.

He shrugs my hands away. "It's fine."

I may not have a lot of experience in relationships, but I know when the other person says *it's fine,* nothing is ever really fine. Not wanting to push him on this right now, I change the subject. "I'm excited to meet your friends." This will be my first time meeting anyone in Krew's social group.

"They're going to like you." He looks up from his phone and trails his eyes up and down my body. "A lot. And I'm going to like you with them." I tilt my head to the side, confused by his statement. "You wanted to earn money, right?"

"Yes," I say hesitantly.

"You'll have your first chance to do that tonight."

The food arrives just minutes before his friends do. I'm setting the containers on the table when the door opens, and a man and woman walk in.

"You're late," Krew says when he sees the couple.

"Talk to this one." The man points to the woman. "She took forever getting ready."

"It seems to be worth it. Get your ass over here." She walks over to where Krew sits on the couch and straddles his lap. He pulls her to him, kissing her deeply. I stare, shocked, and don't even realize I dropped a glass. It shatters at my feet. Krew pulls away from the woman and gives me a look.

"I'm sorry. I'll clean it up." I hurry to get the broom and dustpan, ensuring every sliver is up off the floor.

"What's his problem?" the man asks as he pulls out a wobbly kitchen chair and sits. The woman leaves Krew's lap to join him at the table.

"I might've forgotten to mention a few details about tonight." They both laugh and start serving their plates.

Uncertain about my role, I turn to the man, extending my hand. "I'm Leo. Nice to meet you." He makes no move to return the gesture, leaving me slightly embarrassed as I drop my arm.

"This one has pristine manners." He motions with his fork.

Turning to Krew for an explanation, I silently hope he clarifies the situation. "Sit down and eat, Leo," he instructs. I obery, lowering into my chair. "That's Dion, and this is Fawn." She glances at Krew and bites her lower lip. "What do you think of my new friend, Fawn?"

"He's cute," she says, her eyes not leaving Krew's.

"You're going to have fun with him tonight, aren't you?" She nods. "See, Leo, I told you they'd like you."

I look between the three of them, feeling like an outsider. The way Krew kissed her tells me they've been together before. He didn't tell me he was bi or that he was involved with anyone else. "I don't understand. You told me you don't share."

"I don't." He takes a bite of his sweet and sour chicken.

"Then what was that?"

"What did it look like?" I'm speechless, so he continues, "Fawn came to play tonight."

"Play?" My voice cracks, and Krew rolls his eyes.

"Fuck." He pins me with his stare. "You said you wanted to work for me. To earn your own money, right?"

"I. Uh." I have no idea what's going on or why the rules suddenly seem to have changed.

"You need to loosen up. Go grab us some beers." Silently, I walk across the kitchen, my head spinning, and open the fridge to grab four cold brown bottles. "Now sit and eat before it's time for you to work," Krew says before turning his attention to Dion.

The men have a cryptic conversation while I pick at the food on my plate, wondering what's going on and what Krew will have me do tonight. It doesn't take long before the answer to my question becomes apparent.

Krew motions to Fawn. She stands and saunters around the table, swaying her hips before she settles on her knees between his spread legs.

I watch as she undoes Krew's pants and wraps her red lips around his dick.

"Jealous?" Dion leans over and asks me quietly.

The roiling in the pit of my stomach tells me that, yes, I'm very jealous. "I thought she was here with you." My voice is quiet. "That she was your girlfriend."

"Unlike my good friend here," Dion chuckles as he motions to Krew. "I like to share my things."

"Take care of my friend," Krew says.

"What?" I ask, shocked.

"You wanted to work for me. Get on your damn knees and let him fuck your mouth."

Dion opens his pants and pulls out his cock. I look over my shoulder at Krew, whose hand is wrapped in Fawn's long red hair while she bobs her head up and down on his length.

My body moves without my consent until I realize I'm on my knees between Dion's long legs.

Dion leans over and says quietly, "If you're a good boy, maybe I'll let you sample her too."

"I don't. I'm not." The words are barely out of my mouth before Dion grabs my head. "Open," he says a second before pushing me down on his cock. Krew's taught me how to relax my throat so I don't gag.

Everything happens in a blur as Dion lifts his hips, keeping a fast and almost frantic pace. On the other side of the table, I hear Krew groan, and my heart breaks knowing he's orgasming in Fawn's mouth. I suck harder, not out of pleasure, but to get this over with faster. Dion slams my face down over and over. His movements become erratic as he grunts. His cock spasms shooting cum down my throat.

He pulls out, and I sit back on my heels to catch my breath.

"You taught this one well," Dion says as he tucks himself back into his pants.

"Come here, Leo," Krew calls me. I stand on shaky legs and go to him. "I want to watch you with Fawn." I open my mouth to protest, but he holds his finger up. "You don't want to disappoint me, do you?"

I should feel angry, but instead, I crave his approval even more. "No."

"Take your clothes off. Let them see you." He points to Fawn, who slides her short, tight dress over her head. She's not wearing anything underneath. I quickly turn my head away. "She's fucking hot, and she's willing to pleasure you. The least you can do is be grateful." Krew points to the couch. "Take him over and undress him."

Wordlessly, Fawn takes my hand and leads me to the sofa. She turns me to face her and stands on her tiptoes to kiss me. She traces the seam of my lips with her tongue, but when I don't open, she moves away and begins taking my clothes off.

I take in her delicate form. Her breasts are small, and her nipples are tight. My eyes travel lower over her flat stomach and curvy hips to her waxed pussy. She sees me looking at her and smiles seductively. When she has my pants off, she puts her hand on my chest and gently pushes me back so I'm lying on the couch.

Despite her obvious physical beauty, her kisses and touches do nothing to arouse me. She takes my flaccid cock into her mouth, trying her best to make me hard, but my body isn't responding.

"Does he need some help?" Krew asks as he comes over. I see something shiny in his hand.

A surge of memories flashes in my mind, sending my heart rate skyrocketing. "No, Krew, please," I beg.

"This will make you feel good," Krew croons.

"I'll get hard. Just give me—" The needle pricks my arm, and a cold liquid shoots into my vein.

Fawn crawls up my legs and straddles my body. She brings her hands to her breasts, rolling her nipples between her fingers as she rubs her pussy over me. It doesn't take long before I feel my cock get hard. She moans seductively as she wraps her hand around me and lowers herself down. With my cock inside her, she leans forward, her breasts flattening against my chest. Her lips meet mine, coaxing my mouth open.

I've never been turned on by a woman, but whatever Krew gave me has lust running through my veins, and my hips move of their own accord. I no longer have control of myself. I exist for one reason—to seek relief inside Fawn's tight, wet body.

"Fuck her, Leo," Krew says. "I want to see you enjoy her."

Any doubts or inhibitions I had before are gone, and I'm left only feeling what's happening at this moment. I grab her hips and move her body up and down faster, harder, chasing my release. Fawn reaches between her legs and plays with her clit while I continue to fuck her. Feral noises fill the room, and I realize they're coming from me. My release comes out of nowhere, taking me by surprise as it explodes through me. I squeeze my eyes shut from the intensity. Fawn cries out as her body squeezes my cock, drawing out my own pleasure.

When I open my eyes, I see Krew and Dion have their phones out. "What are you doing?" I attempt to shield Fawn's body with my own.

"You insisted on wanting to work for me." Krew narrows his eyes. "This video will make us a pretty penny."

Fawn climbs off me and looks between the men. "You did

good, sweetheart," Dion compliments her. "You can have your pick who you want next."

"Both of you," she says sweetly.

"That can be arranged."

"Get this place cleaned up," Krew orders as he lifts Fawn over his shoulder. She laughs as he smacks her ass. "You can come join us when you're done."

Leopold

"Get up," Krew says, startling me awake.

After cleaning up last night, I settled on the couch, grappling with what to do next. Ramiro's contact was pulled up, but uncertainty gripped me. I must've fallen asleep because now the sun is shining brightly. Pushing myself into a sitting position, I search for my phone, my hands moving between the cushions.

"Looking for this?" Krew holds up my phone.

"Yes." I stand up, my body cracking and popping from the odd sleeping position. "I don't think this is working out between us. I'm going to call Ra—"

Krew drops my phone on the floor in front of him and steps on it with his black leather biker boots. The plastic and glass crush under the weight. My stomach sinks.

"I was content to care for you and keep you for myself," Krew says, running his knuckles down my cheek. Instead of it being comforting, it sends chills down my spine. "But you insisted on wanting to work for and earn your own money."

"I was wrong."

"You should've listened to me when I said you didn't have to." He points to the broken phone. "Clean this up. I have guests coming shortly." When I don't move, he yells, "Now."

I hurry to sweep up the remnants of my phone. Fear courses through my body at the realization that this now useless device was my only connection to anyone outside of this apartment. I should've called Ramiro last night. I was stupid to let my guard down and fall asleep. Now, I'm on my own.

I was so deep in my thoughts that I didn't see Krew make us a plate of leftovers from last night's takeout. He's sitting at the table eating when I go over to him. "I'm going to get my things and go."

"Look, Leo," Krew says, lowering his voice. "I should've told you what I hoped for last night. I like to have a good time with Dion and Fawn. You can't blame a guy for that, right?"

"Of course not," I say, trying to appease him. "It's just not my thing."

He raises his hands. "Fair enough. Sit down and eat."

"I don't think that's a good idea."

"You barely touched your food last night. You must be starving." He kicks my chair out with his foot. "Have a bite to eat while we talk. If you still want to go after that, we'll figure it out from there." I don't move. "I'm not a bad guy, Leo. You know that. And we're good together. I don't want what happened last night to come between us."

"What about my phone?"

"That was a stupid move on my part. I'll buy you a new one. Now, have some lunch with me." Even though I still feel uneasy, I am hungry, so I sit. "That's my boy." Krew's praise still causes my stomach to flutter.

"What are you going to do with that video from last night?"

"Dion and I run a website," he says between bites. "We make a killing from videos like that. You and Fawn looked fucking hot together. It'll get a ton of views and bring in a lot of money." I don't look up while I chew. "It's nothing to be ashamed of, Leo."

"I'm not," I say quickly. "I just don't think I'm comfortable doing that sort of thing."

"I sell sex, Leo." He shrugs. "You didn't have to be a part of it.

I was content to keep you for myself, but that wasn't good enough for you."

I see his mouth moving, but his words are beginning to slur. "What's happening?"

"I put a little something in your food," he says as if it's nothing. "It'll make you feel lighter and much more agreeable." I grab my head, trying to stop the feeling. Krew stands up and comes over to me. "You like to please me, don't you, baby?"

"Yes." Tears drip down my cheeks

"That's my good boy." He wraps me in his arms, and I rest my head against his chest. "This is how you please me." I feel a familiar stick in my arm.

"No," I cry.

"Shh," he whispers as he strokes my hair.

"I don't want this."

"Give it a few minutes, and you'll feel much different."

"What did you give—? I can't form words.

Time seems to stretch as everything moves in slow motion. Krew's voice reaches my ears, but the words are a blur.

Pain. Splitting. Burning. I try to fight to get away, but strong hands hold onto my waist. That's when I realize someone's inside me, thrusting hard. I cry out. Krew's hand grab's my hair and pulls my head up as a cock slides into my mouth. "Be a good boy and show them how well I've trained you, and maybe I'll even let you come."

I gag on the dick hitting the back of my throat. I don't want this. I don't want any of this. The man behind me thrusts furiously. He grunts as a warm sensation spurts all over my back. Seconds after, the man fucking my face releases down my throat.

Krew pushes me off to the side, and my head hits the floor. I don't move while I try to catch my breath.

My entire body throbs with pain, and I notice a trickle of blood running down my leg.

"What's wrong?" A fat man with brown curly hair stoops in front of me. I'm so tired I can barely lift my head. "Are you jealous that you're not being fucked right now?" His cackling fills the air, and the stench of his rancid breath hits me square in the face.

In a shaky voice, I utter, "No." My head feels clouded, and the surroundings are unrecognizable, leaving me utterly clueless about what's happening.

"No? Your dick doesn't seem to agree with you. Billy, get your ass over here," He calls over his shoulder. "Our boy here wants to fuck it. He's earned a little reward." The guy grabs my arm in an attempt to pull me to my feet.

"Let me go," I plead, attempting to pull away, but weakness and lack of coordination hinder my efforts.

"It looks like he might need some more *encouragement*," Krew says, coming into my view.

I grab onto his leg. "Please, help me."

"Hearing you beg turns me on." Krew strokes my dick, and despite not wanting any part of this, his strong hand wrapped around me, pumping up and down, feels so good. I can't help the moan that slips from my lips. "That's right. Tell me how much you like this."

When I don't answer, he stops.

"If you don't tell me, I won't let you come. And you want to come, don't you, Leo?"

Whatever drugs Krew's giving me keeps my body desperate for more. Despite the disgust I feel inside, my physical body can't resist. "I like it," I mumble.

"Louder. Tell the camera how much you like this."

"I like it," I say louder.

Gripping me tightly, Krew starts moving his hand again. My body tenses as my orgasm builds.

"That's right, Leo," Krew whispers. "This is what we've been waiting for. You're doing so good."

I look up and see two of the guys with their dicks in their hands. They're jerking off watching this sick show. I know it's disgusting, but somehow, seeing it turns me on even more, and I groan loudly.

"Come for me," he orders.

My body trembles as I shoot wave after wave of cum over Krew's hand.

"Such a good boy," he croons.

Movement catches my eye. "What's that?"

"A reward." My skin pricks as he pushes a needle in. "Something to keep you feeling good."

It's only seconds before I feel my body falling. The all-too-familiar fog begins to creep back in.

No, not again. When will this hell stop?

Anthony

EXCITEMENT FILLS ME AS I HEAD BACK TO ART CLASS today. In just three weeks, I've found a sense of calm through this creative outlet, as if I've reclaimed a part of myself.

I arrive at the community center early, anticipating setting up my easel and getting started. On my way to the classroom, I stop in the snack room and purchase a bottle of water from the vending machine.

"Tony?" a woman asks from behind me.

I spin around. "Jennifer?"

"What are you doing here?" she asks while balancing a little girl on her hip.

"I'm taking an art class." I step off to the side so I'm not blocking the machine. "I'm surprised to see you here."

"The girls take a tumbling class. They've been out sick for a few weeks, and I guess I'm out of practice. I forgot their water bottles, so I wanted to grab them a drink for during class." I wait while she takes her turn. "How long have you been taking art classes?"

"Come on, Mommy. We're going to be late." The older of the girls tug on her arm.

"Be patient, Anna. We have more than enough time."

"Who's 'dat?" the younger of the girls asks, pointing her chubby finger at me.

"This is Mommy's friend, Tony," she says as she gently lowers her daughter to the floor and takes her hand. "And these are my girls. This is Anna." She pats her older daughter's head. "And this is Chloe Bear."

"I'm not a bear." She giggles.

"It's very nice to meet you both," I say as we step into the hall. "It was nice bumping into you."

"You, too." We start walking and laugh when we go in the same direction. "The girls are in the preschool gym in the back hall."

"I'm going that way, too. If you don't mind, I'll walk with you."

Anna eyes me warily as she clings to her mother's hand. "Do you promise you won't leave?"

"I'll be outside like always."

"Promise?" She looks up, her big blue eyes filling with tears.

"I promise."

"This is my stop," I say when we get to the door of my classroom, which is next door to the preschool gym. "Have fun tumbling."

"It was nice seeing you again," Jennifer says.

"Same to you." Though I know I should head inside and get set up, I can't help but watch as Jennifer tries to drop the girls off. Chloe runs right in, but Anna cries and clings to her mom.

"We come here every week," Jennifer says patiently, getting down to her daughter's eye level. "You love Miss Bry."

"I don't want you to leave," Anna sobs.

"I'll be out here with all the other Mommies."

"Anna," a young gym teacher says, trying to intervene. "Would you like to be the line leader today?"

Big fat tears drip down her cheeks as the little girl takes her teacher's hand and walks into the gym. Jennifer stands up, taking a deep breath, revealing the stress and exhaustion etched on her face.

"Jennifer," I call as I hurry toward her.

She quickly composes herself when she sees me coming. "I'm sorry you had to see that."

"There's no reason to apologize."

"She's had a hard time adjusting to any changes since her father died."

"That's understandable." I know how difficult it was for me to figure out how to navigate life without Kameron. I can't fathom how hard it must've been for Jennifer to explain to two young children why their Daddy wasn't coming home. That's when I get an idea. "How long is the girls' class?"

"An hour, why?" she asks warily.

"Art class is only forty-five minutes. Why don't you come join us?"

"Oh no," she laughs. "I am not an artist."

"There are people of all different skill levels in there. You can let the gym teacher know you'll be in the room next door if they need you."

Jennifer looks between the gym and me. "I don't know."

"There are no naked models in there, I promise," I say with a grin, and she laughs. "Try it once,' I suggest a compromise. "If you hate it, you never have to go back."

"I might regret this, but okay." I wait while she lets the tumbling teacher know she'll be next door. Then she rejoins me.

"Ready?" I ask with a smile.

"As I'll ever be."

Our class consists of ten people, making it the perfect-sized group—large enough not to be overwhelming and small enough not to feel singled out. Jennifer and I choose easels next to each other. Today's lesson is drawing what we see, concentrating on composition and shading. I've never drawn with charcoal on a canvas. It feels good to try something new.

"Have you always lived in the city?" I ask Jen while we work on our sketches.

"It's been about six years. I moved into Jeff's apartment when we got married," she explains. "What about you?"

"I was born and raised here. Wouldn't trade it for anything."

"I grew up in Clearfield. It's a small farming town in Pennsylvania. While Jeff and I were dating, I fell in love with it here." She turns to look at me. "But since September, things haven't been the same."

"Do you have any family close by?"

"No. Jeff's parents passed away a few years ago. I tried to get my mom to come live with us, but she refused to leave her home. We try to visit her as much as possible."

We draw in silence for a few minutes until Jennifer leans over. "Holy shit, Tony," she says a bit too loud, and several heads turn. "Were you an artist in a former life?"

"Something like that." I chuckle. "Let's see yours." I lean over and take a look at her canvas.

"I told you I can't draw," she says as she waves her hand at the smudged drawing in front of her.

"It's not that bad." I walk over to her canvas. "May I?"

"Please."

"If we get rid of this spot." I use my eraser to clean up the reflections in the water. "And add a little shadowing here." I touch up the buildings that line the water's edge. "Then all you need to do is add the trees." I take a step back. "What do you think?"

"I think you're magic." She giggles.

"Nah. I just touched up a few areas. You did the rest on your own."

Before we know it, class is wrapping up for the day. "Thank you so much for inviting me to come with you. It's the most fun I've had in a long time."

"I'm glad you enjoyed it. Maybe you'll consider coming back next week?"

"I really enjoyed myself. I think I will," she says as we walk into the hallway and turns to me. "The girls and I usually go out for an early dinner. Would you like to join us?"

Aside from work and therapy activities, I haven't been out in a long time. "I'd love to."

Anthony

KAMERON'S DEATH LEFT A HOLE IN MY LIFE IN MORE ways than I realized for many months. The incident at my restaurant seemed to be the catalyst I needed to admit I was struggling. I've been regularly attending the grief support group, which has given me a place to safely explore the emotions associated with the loss I experienced. Successfully managing the stages of grief hasn't been easy. Being surrounded by others walking a similar path has made it manageable.

A big part of that healing has been my friendship with Jennifer. We've talked daily since I had dinner with her and the girls a few weeks ago. In a way most others might not understand, some might even call morbid, the fact that we both lost our significant other in the North Tower is comforting. It has allowed us to develop a fast friendship.

We're at Loving Arms when she gets a text. After she reads it, she leans over to me. "It's my sitter. Anna's having a tough time. I'm going to have to leave early."

"I can go with you if you think it might help."

"It certainly won't hurt."

The group knows that Jen's daughter has been struggling, so when she tells them we have to leave, it's met with well wishes.

Jennifer's quiet on the subway ride from the church to her neighborhood in the Village. We walk the last few blocks in silence until we're outside of her building.

"Jeff and I bought this house early last summer. We were so excited to move from our cramped apartment to a three-bedroom home close to the school we wanted the girls to attend." She sighs. "This neighborhood was ideal. Everything was supposed to be perfect."

"I understand having to change the vision for the future."

"I still get angry with Jeff for leaving me alone," she admits, looking up at me. "I didn't want to be a single mother. Jeff was supposed to be here with me."

"I wish I could bring him back," I say, feeling the discomfort of helplessness.

"Nothing is okay right now, Tony. Anna's getting worse," she adds, her hand moving to her chest. "I'm barely holding it together. I'm so tired of being alone."

I wrap my arms around her. "I'll never be a replacement, but I'm more than willing to help however I can."

"I feel like I'm failing them," she cries.

"Don't say that. The girls know you're here for them and love them," I encourage her. "Eventually, it'll get easier," I echo the advice I've often received.

"Did you and Kameron want to have children?" she asks, wiping away the tears.

"We talked about someday, but obviously, that wasn't meant to be." I shrug. "But now I get to spoil your girls," I say, smiling.

"I believe people are put into one another's lives for a reason." She opens the door to her ground-floor apartment.

"Mama," Chloe, wearing her princess pajamas, yells as she races around the corner. "Uncle Tony," she shrieks when she sees me and comes barreling at me.

"It might not be how you originally planned, but there are two little girls here who've adopted you," Jennifer says softly.

Her words warm my heart. "I missed you, Chloe bear," I say as I lift the little girl and give her a hug.

"I'm sorry I had to text you," Rachel, the babysitter, says as we enter the living room, where a sobbing Anna sits on her lap.

"It's okay," Jennifer says, sitting next to her. "You did the right thing."

Anna climbs onto her mom's lap, tears streaming down her face.

"What's wrong, sweetheart?"

"It got dark. You didn't come back."

"We talked about this. I would be gone until after dark, but I'd come back," she explains patiently. "Did you try cuddling your special stuffie?"

"I did, but it didn't help." Anna continues crying. "I was scared."

"Mommy's here now." She holds her little girl tight, trying to console her. "Thank you for keeping them, Rachel. I hope they behaved."

"They're always angels," the young girl says as she stands.

"Are you leaving?" Anna sits up suddenly.

"I have to go home."

"Please don't go," Anna begs, holding onto her babysitter's leg.

She smiles at her young charge. "I'll come back."

"Promise?" She asks, her bottom lip quivering.

Rachel exchanges a worried look with Jennifer, who nods.

"Do you remember what we talked about?" Rachel asks as she crouches down to Anna's level. "I will always do my very best to come back to your house, but I can't make that a promise."

"It's something our family therapist is helping us with," Jennifer whispers. "To not make promises we might not be able to keep."

"That makes a lot of sense." I watch the scene unfolding before me. Anna's crying and rubbing her puffy red eyes.

Looking around, I see the girl's art supplies on a shelf in the corner of the room. "Can I try something?"

"Please."

I walk over to the shelf and grab some paper and a box of crayons. "Do you like to draw?" Anna nods. "So do I." I smile as I sit on the couch next to the girl. "Would you like to draw with me and then, when Rachel comes back next time, you can show her all your pictures?

"What if she doesn't come back?" Anna asks quietly, her voice catching on a sob. "Like my daddy."

"I know how scary that is. I had someone I loved very much not come back, too."

"Were they in the tall building, too?"

"They were."

"That's sad." She swipes at her face.

"It is. But I'm learning how to not be so sad or scared anymore."

"You are?" she asks, releasing Rachel's leg.

"Yep. Do you want to know how?" I ask and set the paper and crayons on the coffee table in front of me.

"Mhm."

"I started drawing pictures. My favorite pictures are of the happy memories I have with the person I loved. When I get sad or scared, I look at them to remind me how to be happy."

"That's such a good idea," Rachel agrees.

I get on my knees next to the table and open the crayon box. "Would you like to draw one with me?"

Anna walks over to me. "Okay."

I put a blank sheet of white paper in front of her and move the crayons between us. Anna takes a blue crayon and starts drawing.

"When I come back next time, will you show me your drawings?"

"Yep," Anna says without looking up.

"I can't wait." Rachel kisses the top of Anna's head. "I'll see you in two days, kiddo."

"Me draw, too," Chloe says as she climbs onto my lap.

I look over my shoulder, and Jennifer mouths *thank you* before she walks Rachel out.

When Jennifer returns, the girls make her sit and draw pictures with us. Time flies, and before I know it, it's almost ten pm.

"It's getting pretty late. I should really get going," I say and get to my feet.

"I didn't realize what time it was," Jennifer adds. "It's way past both of your bedtime."

"Please don't go, Uncle Tony," Anna wraps her arms around my neck.

"It's past my bedtime, too," I say as I squeeze her back.

She releases me and studies my face carefully before saying, "You can sleep here."

"That's very kind." I grin. "But I didn't bring my clothes or my toothbrush."

Anna chews on her lower lip. "Can you come back tomorrow?"

"I have to work tomorrow. But if your mommy says it's okay, I'll come back another day, and we can draw some more."

"Is that okay, Mommy?"

"It's absolutely okay."

"Yay." Anna claps and bounces on her toes.

The girls are happily drawing when we walk out of the room.

"This is the first time since Jeff left us that she hasn't had a meltdown when someone was leaving," Jennifer says as we walk toward her front door.

"I'm glad I was able to help."

"Mommy," Anna yells. "Chloe's eating my crayons."

"Sounds like you're needed in the other room. Thank you for having me over." I hug her goodnight. "I'll call you tomorrow."

<h1 style="text-align:center">Leopold</h1>

STEPPING OUT OF WALKING IN THE LIGHT brought overwhelming relief. I believed the worst was behind me. I trusted the legal system to punish David and the rest of the staff in that horrible place. To make sure all of the boys that were being held hostage there were set free and would be safe. Looking back, that was a naïve thought. Of course, they'd have a story to cover up their crimes. And who'd believe the kid who was placed there by their loving family because of their delinquent behaviors?

But at least I was out and was okay. Safe Haven was the first place I'd ever lived where I was accepted for who I was—no question. Ramiro was the father I'd always longed for. He accepted all of us just as we were. He worked tirelessly, helping us get our education, find jobs, and eventually a place of our own. I lost my chance at a promising future the day I refused to heed Ramiro's warning and chose Krew over him.

Now, I've been reduced to nothing more than a whore to be fucked by whoever walks through Krew's door. There's a constant stream of men and women who show up at all hours of the day and night. Clothes? I haven't worn them in weeks. I suspect that's part of Krew's plan. He keeps me naked and strung out so I can't run. I have no choice but to stay here and be subjected to his sick plans.

Whatever poison Krew's pumping through me ensures I don't ever fully lose consciousness. At least when the drugs are at their height, the almost non-stop sex is a relief. It's when they begin to wear off that I realize I'm trapped—a slave to my treacherous body. Thankfully, whenever that happens, Krew is there with his needle in my vein. The clear liquid is a relief. It silences my thoughts once again.

"He won't get hard," a stick-thin woman with rotting teeth says. "How is he supposed to fuck me if he's like this." She motions to my deflated dick.

"Maybe he's not into you," Krew snickers.

I know he's been making me take Viagara. I've swallowed so many little blue pills I lost count. At some points, he gave me so much that no matter how many times I orgasmed, my dick stayed painfully hard. I'm not into women, especially this one, but that's never stopped my body's physical reaction before. As long as he feeds me the drug, my dick stands at attention for whoever's here, but even though I took them a few hours ago, nothing's happening.

"He's fucked me before," she whines. "Can't you give him something else?"

"I already gave him shit that should work." He walks away.

She marches over to Krew, not caring that she's fully naked. "I paid good money for this."

"You paid for time with him. I can't guarantee results," he snickers.

"I'll take you then." She reaches out to undo Krew's pants, but he grabs her wrist.

"Don't touch me," he warns, his voice lethally dark.

She crosses her arms across her nearly flat chest. "I want my money back."

"I don't give refunds, sweetheart," Krew lights a joint. "Put your clothes on and get the fuck out."

"What?"

"You heard me." He picks up her clothes and tosses them at her. "You've overstayed your welcome. Get out."

She pulls her dingy T-shirt over her head and slides her stretched-out yoga pants up her bony legs before giving Krew the finger and slamming the door behind her.

"You're lucky that wasn't one of my important clients," Krew snarls. "What the hell is wrong with you?"

I pull my knees against my chest, trying to preserve some warmth, but don't answer him. I've learned to stay quiet when he's in this kind of mood.

"I have to do a quick run to restock." He stabs the joint out on the cracked Formica counter and kicks some trash out of the way. "This place is a dump. When I get back, it better be cleaned up and ready for tonight." He squats down to make eye contact with me. "You have a very important guest coming this evening." I make the mistake of lifting my head to meet his eyes. "That got your attention. Do you want to know who it is?"

"No," I say quietly.

I don't care who's coming. One body is the same as the next. All of them are unwanted. I begin to tremble as the drugs start to wear off.

Krew stands back up, and I assume he's going to get a needle, but instead, he walks toward the door.

"Can I have a shot before you go?" I ask, desperate for relief.

"No." Krew stops with his hand on the doorknob. "This client has requested you to be present. He prefers you to fight him."

He prefers me to fight him? I've never resisted any of Krew's so-called clients.

I watch as he reaches out and turns the handle. "David can't wait to see you again." The door slams behind him.

Silence.

My brain struggles to digest Krew's words.

David?

When I finally comprehend his words, fear sets in. I don't know how long I've been here or how many people have used my body. Their names and faces mean nothing to me as long as Krew keeps my mind numb. But I won't survive being raped by David again.

I don't know what to do. How to get out of my current situation.

When I woke up after the first time Krew drugged me, I wasn't in his apartment anymore. I'm pretty sure we're in the same building, just one of the other empty apartments. This one has a solid steel door like Krew's place, but there's no lock on the inside. The times Krew leaves, the door is locked from the outside. There are windows, but they have bars trapping me inside.

I grab the cushion of the couch and struggle to get on my feet. Even though it's futile, I stumble to the door and shake it. I'm not surprised when it doesn't budge. I search the mostly empty space, frantically looking for anything I can use to help me escape.

"Dammit," I yell when I find nothing.

My body shakes so hard that my teeth rattle. My escape efforts are now combined with desperation for more drugs. I've watched where Krew gets the vials from, but the cupboard has a padlock on it. I punch the wood so hard that my knuckles bust open, and blood drips down my arm.

I try the doors to the two other rooms but find them all locked. The only one that opens leads to the bathroom. Lying on the floor, I see one of Krew's black T-shirts. Sliding it over my head, I'm thankful for the little bit of clothing offering warmth to my body.

Tearing open the medicine cabinet on the wall, I'm disappointed to find it empty. My heart pounds against my ribs as if it's trying to get out of my body. I grab the sides of my head and scream, hoping it stops my torment. That's when I look up and notice the small window without bars.

It's a fixed window, so I know my only hope of getting out is to break the glass. There's a worn towel lying in the bottom of the stand-up shower. I grab it and wrap it around my fist, hoping it provides some protection. It takes several tries before the glass finally shatters. Using the towel, I wipe away the shards as best as I can. Slivers of glass are embedded in my bare feet as I try to hoist myself up, but I'm weak from the lack of nutrition and the drugs.

My vision blurs in and out as I stumble back through the dark hallway to the kitchen and grab one of the metal folding chairs. It takes my remaining strength to drag it back to the bathroom. I climb onto the chair and am close enough to slide one leg through the small opening. As I fold my body to fit through, shards of glass I miss slice my skin, but I don't care. Freedom is just on the other side.

It's dark as my foot searches for something, anything, to steady me. But there's nothing there. My grasp on what's left of the windowsill slips, and I fall from the second floor. The dead remnants of a bush slow my body's fall to the ground. Even still, I land on my left arm.

Slowly, I push up, keeping my injured arm cradled against me as I catch my breath. I remain still, listening for any hint that people are outside the building, but there's nothing. Knowing I need to get out of here before Krew returns, I drag myself to my feet and walk as fast as my weary body will take me. I don't know exactly where I'm going other than away from this neighborhood.

Leopold

SILENTLY MOVING THROUGH THE SHADOWS, I COVER what feels like miles until the lights of a corner store become visible. I contemplate if it's too close to Krew's building to gamble on whoever might be inside, but there's no other option. I won't last much longer. If I collapse on the street, the odds of being saved are slimmer than the risk I take going inside.

Clad in a T-shirt that provides minimal coverage, I cautiously watch for a few minutes, waiting until the parking lot is empty. I hope to make it inside without causing too much of a scene. Once I'm relatively sure the store is empty, I step out from behind the corner of the building, which provides me shelter. I hurry across the street and slip inside the store.

The door beeps, and the girl behind the counter looks up. "Oh my God," she yells.

"Please," I stumble and grasp onto the counter to keep me upright. "I need help."

She steps back but doesn't take her eyes off me. "What do you want?"

"Could you make a call for me?" I cast a worried glance over my shoulder, afraid Krew or one of his friends would have realized I was gone or followed me and are ready to drag me back.

"Um." She chews on her lower lip. "Is it your dealer or something?"

"No. I'm not..." I look down at myself and see what she's seeing. "His name is Ramiro Vega."

Cautiously, she pulls her cell phone out from under the counter. For a second, I'm afraid she's calling the police, and I consider running. Then, she says, "What's his number?"

"I don't know." My head falls.

"I'll try searching his name," she says.

A car pulls into the parking lot, and my pulse kicks into overdrive. "I can't let them find me. Would you hide me?" I steal another glance when the car door closes. "Please?"

She looks from me to whoever's outside the door. "I might end up regretting this, but come on." She motions for me to go behind the counter.

I move as fast as possible and drop to the ground, curling up as small as possible. The door beeps. She briefly looks up but then resumes scrolling on her cell phone, a move that doesn't attract any attention.

The back-and-forth of two male voices catches my attention. One unmistakably belongs to Krew. I lower my head, pulling my legs closer, silently pleading with the universe to be on my side.

The girl discreetly slides her phone under the counter as they come nearer, and items are placed on the counter. "Are you ready to say yes to my offer, sweetheart?"

"Fuck off, Krew," she says as she punches numbers into the cash register.

The door beeps again.

"I'd like to fuck you," Krew says crudely, and both men laugh.

"Is that so?" A third man joins the conversation. "What are you doing in my neighborhood?"

"We were just passing through and got thirsty." More snickering.

"Lindsay told me you've been sniffing around." His voice grows louder as his feet come into view. He casts a downward glance, his dark stare briefly locking onto mine. Without showing any reaction, he looks back up. "You know you don't belong here, Krew. This is the only warning you're going to get. The next time I find out you're on my streets, you won't be leaving alive."

"The offer stands, sweetheart," Krew says.

Click.

My glance shifts upward, and I see the man holding a small black handgun.

"Come on, Krew. We don't need any trouble."

"You should listen to your friend," the man with the gun says.

The door opens. "Let's go."

The man doesn't replace the gun's safety until tires squeal and the sound of a car fades. Then he slides the gun into the holster on his waistband. "You okay, Linz?"

"Yeah," she says. "I don't think he is, though." She points in my direction.

"Who the hell is this?"

"I don't know," she says softly. "He stumbled in a few minutes before they did."

"What's your name?"

"Leopold," I stammer.

"Are you high?"

"Maybe?"

"Get up." He grabs my shirt by the collar, dragging me to my feet.

"He's hurt and needs help," the girl pleads, grabbing his arm.

"I don't want any drug-addicted losers in here—"

"No. Please," I beg. "I can't go back to Krew."

The guy freezes but doesn't let go of the T-shirt. "What are you talking about?"

"He asked me to call someone named Ramiro Vega," she adds.

"Vega? From Safe Haven?" he asks, pinning me with his stare.

I nod.

"Get him into the back room," he instructs the girl. "I have a call to make."

Anthony

TONIGHT'S THE GRAND OPENING FOR *Italiano Desiderio.* Owen's outside and has texted me that the line extends down the block and around the corner. We're opening in less than five minutes. I've gathered my staff for a final pep talk before we open the doors.

"It's going to get busy in a few minutes. I've been in your shoes and know the nerves you're experiencing right now," I say as I look at the eager faces of my employees. "I have faith in every one of you. We're going to continue working as a team and show this city what authentic Italian cuisine is all about. Are you ready?" A resounding chorus of yeses and applause fills the room. "Let's do this."

The group disperses to their stations, and I walk to the front doors, opening them wide. "Thank you all for your patience," I address the waiting crowd. "I'd like to welcome you to *Italiano Desiderio.*" I step inside and watch the first of my patrons enter.

I'm thankful for all the familiar faces in the sea of people.

"Congratulations, Tony," Alex shakes my hand. "This place is gorgeous."

"Thank you for coming." I turn to Raina. "Please seat Alex in the back room with my other personal guests."

"Right this way," she says, batting her eyes at him.

"Uncle Tony," Anna calls as she wraps her tiny arms around my waist.

"There's one of my favorite little girls." I swoop her into my arms, making her giggle.

"I can't believe all the people out there," Jennifer says as she kisses my cheek.

"It's unreal." I set Anna down. "I can't believe it's finally happening," I confess.

"I'm so proud of you." Jennifer beams.

Anna tugs on my pant leg. "Mommy says we're on an all-girls date tonight."

"She did, did she?" I chuckle.

"Mhm."

"Where's Chloe?"

"Rachel offered to keep her," Jennifer explains.

"I'll make sure you get an extra scoop of ice cream with your dessert," I whisper, winking at Anna.

"Yay," she cheers and claps her hands.

"Raina," I say when my hostess returns. "Please escort this little princess and her Mom to the back room."

The topic of my involvement in the BDSM lifestyle wasn't on the agenda to discuss with Jennifer. However, I had to spill the beans when Star texted during our afternoon at Chelsea Market, asking for help with the club's food delivery. Reluctantly, I shared everything with Jennifer on our way to the club. To my surprise, she was unfazed by my revelation.

Since then, Jen's gotten to know my closest friends from the club. While she's not interested in the lifestyle, she's open and accepting of all of them—especially Alex. Although he's made it clear, he's not interested in a woman in or out of the lifestyle.

Several hours pass before the line outside dissipates, and the number of diners inside starts to decrease. My team has been troopers. They're exhausted, but they keep pushing and are giving our customers an excellent experience. Owen has also worked tirelessly. He's dedicated the entire night to managing the crowd and engaging with guests waiting for their tables.

"I'd say tonight was an overwhelming success," he says, giving my shoulder a reassuring squeeze.

"I was afraid no one would come out. I'm absolutely stunned," I confess. I'm hit with a familiar sadness. "I just wish Kam were here to see this."

"I have no doubt he is," Owen says with certainty. He gestures to the framed drawing on the wall of the Twin Towers, standing majestically with an angel in an FDNY uniform above them with outstretched arms. "That's a beautiful picture. Who's the artist?"

No one knows that I draw. It's been a secret of mine. I pause for a second before responding. "I am.'"

Owen's eyes grow wide. "I knew you were a master with wax. I had no idea you were a bona fide artist."

A laugh escapes me at his words. "I'm not sure I'd use the term *artist* for myself." I open up to Owen about the art class I'm taking and how it has become a grounding force for me. "I've missed being able to express myself with wax."

"I know things haven't been easy for you since Kam passed," Owen says.

"I have to thank you for the come-to-Jesus talk in the ER. If it wasn't for you, I would've fallen deeper into the black hole I was in."

"I'd like to take all the credit," he smiles, a hint of modesty in his expression. "But all I did was make a suggestion. You've done the rest."

I've been blessed with friends who courageously share the difficult truths. Individuals who supported and loved me through my darkest days. Because of them, I'm standing here tonight as a man who's no longer afraid of what tomorrow may bring.

Anthony

Time was once divided into B.C. and A.D. Now, we distinguish between pre-9/11 and post-9/11. The era of visiting historical monuments without walking through metal detectors is long gone. Boarding a plane is no longer as straightforward as rushing to the gate at the last minute. Passengers must now arrive early at security checkpoints, where they go through the process of removing shoes, emptying pockets, and having bags scanned by high-powered X-ray machines. The world as we once knew it has been irrevocably changed.

September 11, 2002. It's exactly one year since that fateful day when the world lost 2,801 innocent lives. The day I lost Kameron. I've experienced so many emotions in the days leading up to today as I've reminisced about the last days Kam and I spent together and how happy we were.

Last night was one of the hardest nights I've endured. President Bush and his wife, Laura, laid a wreath at Ground Zero. Many of the gathered family members and I had the opportunity to speak with the President and First Lady. It was an emotional night for everyone in attendance.

When I arrived back home, I had a panic attack. I couldn't remember what Kameron's voice sounded like. I feared losing the saved voice messages from him and never being able to hear him speaking to me. What if I forget what he looks like? How his amber eyes sparkled when we were together. It was the first time I called Pastor Andrea and Kelly outside of a group meeting. They spent several hours on the phone helping me feel the feelings but not letting them rule me. Being afraid or sad is okay, but I don't have to stay there.

This morning, Jennifer and I, along with Owen and Star, arrived at Ground Zero with thousands of others to pay tribute to the lives lost as a result of the senseless tragedy. Amidst arriving family and friends of the victims, we reverently place photographs and flowers at the site where the World Trade Center once stood. The haunting notes of Amazing Grace, played by bagpipers, wafts on the breeze, adding a poignant touch to the atmosphere.

Mayor Bloomberg opens the solemn ceremony, pausing for a moment of silence at 8:46 am, the exact time the first plane hit the North Tower. Former Mayor Giuliani begins reading the names of the victims. At 9:03, silence once again falls over the gathered crowd, and bells chime, marking the time the second hijacked plane struck the south tower.

Fifty-six minutes later, bells chime, marking the South Tower's collapse. Finally, at 10:29 am, the moment I've been dreading, we silently memorialize the collapse of the North Tower.

Jennifer grabs my hand for support. Despite my efforts, my heart splits open, and tears flow uncontrollably as Owen and Star wrap us in their protective embrace. The pain is just as visceral today as it was when I stood in my kitchen, Kameron and I expressing our love to one another in his final moments of life.

The reading of the names lasts for almost three hours. As the soul-stirring melody of Taps played on the trumpet drifts through the air, I close my eyes and allow memories to wash over me.

The tingling rush of excitement when I spotted him leaning against the wall, biting his bottom lip, waiting for me the night I met him.

His laughter was an infectious melody that held the power to brighten even the gloomiest of days.

The profound moment when he lowered to his knees, offering me the most precious gift—his submission.

His lips, soft and tender, caressing mine in a whisper of shared intimacy.

An unspoken commitment, a love that saw beyond imperfections, painting a portrait where each perceived flaw was a stroke contributing to the masterpiece of our relationship.

Our promises of forever—cruelly snatched away by a heartless twist of fate.

Until we are reunited again, amore mio.

Leopold

The door opens, and the man who chased Krew away returns. In his hands are a hot coffee and a wrapped sandwich

"You look like you could use something to eat," he says as he sets the food on the desk. I eye it warily. "It's sealed. I didn't tamper with it."

Greedily, I grab it, examining it from all angles, before ripping off the wrapper and taking a big bite. My mouth is dry, and I choke when I attempt to swallow.

"The coffee's safe, too," he encourages. When I don't reach for it, he opens the door. "Linz, grab a bottle of water from the cooler, would ya?"

"Sure."

A moment later, she opens the door and passes him the water. "Let me know when Vega gets here," he says and closes the door softly. "Here." He passes me the cold bottle.

"Thank you." I turn the cap, relieved to hear the crack of the plastic seal, and drink half of it in one gulp.

"So, Leopold," he says as he leans against the desk, watching me carefully. "Judging by your reaction to Krew, I take it he's involved in what's going on with you."

I take the last bite of the cold-cut sandwich and lick my fingers so I don't waste even the tiniest crumb.

"With all those marks," he says, pointing to my arms. "I'm going to assume you're a client of his, and he cut you off."

"No. Krew was my boyfriend, or so I thought," I say quietly and then finish the water bottle, hoping it soothes my dry, scratchy throat. "Then something happened. He changed."

"Did he happen to pick you up at *Prism?*" the guy inquires, and I nod. "That's his usual MO."

I try to wrap my head around this new information. "He's done this before?" I ask.

"He has," the man says. "Most of the boys he brings back disappear. How did you get away?"

"I broke the bathroom window. It was the only one without bars," I add.

"You're lucky."

I glance at the door. "Can I have another water?"

"Sure," he says, one side of his mouth lifting in a smile. "I'll be right back."

After the man disappears from the office, I bring my legs onto the chair and wrap the T-shirt around them, trying to generate warmth. My head drops onto my knees, and my eyelids gently droop shut.

The door opening causes me to jump, and I nearly fall off the chair.

"Hey there," the man says, grabbing my arm. "No one's going to hurt you here."

"Where is here, and who are you?" I ask and then slap my hand over my mouth at my brazenness.

"You're fine." He passes me the plastic bottle. "My name's Donnie. This is my store."

Before I can ask any more questions, there's a soft knock on the door. "Who is it?"

"It's me," the female voice says. "Mr. Vega's here."

Donnie opens the office door. "Come on in."

"Leo," Ramiro says, brushing past Donnie and hurrying over to me. "What happened to you?"

"I'll give you two a few minutes. I'm going to lock up the front," Donnie says, then disappears.

"I didn't think you'd come," I whisper, tears streaming down my face.

"Absolutely, I wouldn't hesitate to come," he says, placing neatly folded clothes on the desk. He then envelops me in a protective embrace. "I'm thankful you had them call me." Ramiro let's go and studies my condition. Opening the door, he calls, "Donnie?"

"What do you need?"

"Can I buy some first aid supplies? I want to try to clean him up some."

"You're not buying anything," Donnie says, returning to the office. Opening a cabinet, he pulls out a first aid kit and passes it to Ramiro. "Some of those cuts look deep. He might need stitches."

"No hospital or doctors. I'm fine." I go to stand up, and the room spins. Ramiro catches me and lowers me back onto the chair.

"Take it easy, Leo." He opens the kit and takes out some alcohol pads. "These are going to sting." My hand jerks from his when the cleaner hits my busted knuckles.

Lindsay appears in the doorway. "I can help with that," she offers.

"Thanks, but I've got it."

"Are you still hungry? I can get you something else to eat." She looks at me expectantly.

I nod appreciatively, "Yes, please."

"When's the last time he fed you?" Donnie asks, and I shrug. "This is the last time that bastard is going to do this. I'm going to kill him."

Ramiro finishes putting a bandaid over one of the more minor cuts before addressing Donnie. "I hate the guy as much as you, but killing him is only going to land you in prison. Leo's free. Once I get him cleaned up, I'll call the police and let—"

"For fuck's sake, Vega. The police won't do shit, and you know it."

Ramiro shakes his head and returns his focus to me. "You're shivering. Let's get you dressed, and then you can drink the coffee to warm up." He holds my arm, steadying me as I slide on the soft sweatpants. "Sit down, and I'll help you change your shirt."

"He's not cold," Donnie says, leaning against the wall. "He's going through withdrawal."

"Leo is not an addict," Ramiro says, coming to my defense.

He motions with his chin. "His arms tell a different story."

"Donnie's right," I say, my voice small.

Ramiro's head shoots over to me. "You started using?" he asks in a hushed tone.

"It wasn't by choice," I say, and a fresh wave of tears falls. "Krew kept me drugged, but I haven't had anything all day."

"What else did he do to you?" Ramiro asks.

I look between him and Lindsay, who's standing in the doorway holding a cup of microwave macaroni and cheese.

"Thanks," Donnie says and takes the food. "Can you wait in the store, please?"

"Sure." She looks at me with tears in her eyes. "Let me know if you need anything." Lindsay leaves the room, closing the door softly behind her.

With my head feeling fuzzy and my thoughts challenging to piece together, I do my best to tell them even a little of what happened. While attempting to recall details, my eyes start to close.

"That's enough, Leo. You're exhausted," Ramiro interrupts gently. "Let's get you home."

"Vega, can we talk for a minute?"

I put my head down on the desk as they move to the back corner of the room. Despite my closed eyes, I can hear their hushed conversation.

"Are you bringing him to Safe Haven?"

"He lost his room there, so I can't," Ramiro says quietly. "I'm going to bring him to my house."

"Withdrawal's going to be a bitch. You don't want your wife and kids to see that."

"What else am I going to do?"

"I'll bring him to my place," Donnie offers. "It's not the first time I've seen someone go through withdrawal."

"This kid's been through a lot. Everyone in his life has betrayed him," he explains. "I don't know if he'll go with you."

"In his current condition, he doesn't have much choice."

There's a long pause before Ramiro says, "I'll call my wife and let her know I'm going to be staying at your place for a few nights."

"You sure about that?"

"Positive."

Leopold

Donnie and Lindsay flank my sides as Lindsay holds the door to the apartment open with her foot. Movement is excruciating. My muscles are already cramping from the lack of drugs.

"Can you give me something?" I grab Donnie's arm, desperate for relief. "Anything?"

"The next few days are going to be fucking hell," he says. "If I give you drugs, it's only going to prolong it."

Sweat drips from my forehead as I shuffle up the concrete steps.

"Where's Ramiro?" I strain to look over my shoulder for the only person I know I can trust.

"Vega went back to his house to grab a few things," Donnie explains patiently as he helps me sit on his grey leather sofa." Linsday's getting the guest room made up for you. I want you to be as comfortable as possible while you're here."

"Is comfort even going to be possible?" I ask, already knowing the answer.

"Not at first," he answers frankly. "It'll get better, though."

"Why are you helping me? What do you want?" Skepticism clouds my judgment. "I hope I didn't offend you."

"No offense taken." He offers me a kind smile. "Make no mistake, I'm not a good guy. I allow drugs and weapons to be bought and sold on my streets. Some people say I'm worse than Krew. Who knows. Maybe they're right." He shrugs. "But one thing I'll never condone is taking unsuspecting people and using them to further his prostitution and trafficking rings."

"Trafficking?"

"Krew lures in young girls or guys, making them believe he's interested in a relationship," Donnie explains, pausing as I absorb his words. ""Then, he blindsides them and keeps them drugged. Usually, they vanish. You're the exception. I'm hoping you can shed some light on what else happens."

It takes me a few seconds to find the right words. "He said he was inviting friends over. I thought it was for dinner or something, but it was for sex." My body starts trembling again as a wave of nausea washes over me. "Everything happened so fast. I didn't see the needle coming. You have to believe me," I beg as the pain in my temples threatens to split my skull into two. I grab the sides of my head as tears blur my vision.

"How about we pick this up when you're feeling better?" Donnie suggests.

"Okay," I mumble.

"Come on." He helps me to my feet. "Let's get you to your room so you can lie down and try to get some sleep."

⸙

Sitting up quickly, a moment of disorientation washes over me. The room is filled with screams, and it takes a minute to comprehend that the agonized sounds are coming from me.

"Make it stop," I yell and dig at my arms and legs. "There's so many. Oh my God. Please make them go away."

"It's okay, Leo," Ramiro says gently, attempting to still my fingers that dig into my skin. "There's nothing there."

"Yes, there is," I argue, fighting his hold on me.

"It's just drugs coming out of your system."

"I can feel them." I continue to struggle.

"Your mind is a powerful thing." He tightens his grasp, remaining patient when he says, "But you're stronger than the drugs, Leo. I need you to take some slow, deep breaths and try to relax. Okay?"

One second, I'm freezing and shivering uncontrollably. The next, I'm trying to rip my clothes off because I'm burning up from the inside out. My body is entirely out of control. Currently, I'm sitting on the bathroom floor, my head hanging over the toilet as I empty what little I've swallowed over the past few days.

"It hurts so badly," I sob.

"I know it does," Donnie says, rubbing small circles on my back.

He and Ramiro have taken turns in my room, ensuring I'm never alone. Lindsay is never far, either. She makes sure they have food, and I have soup and smoothies.

"I can't do this anymore," I say as I slump over on the floor, breathless.

"You can and you will." His tone leaves no room for argument, not that I have the energy to do so. "You have no choice, Leo. Do you hear me? I won't let you give up."

I push my weary body off the floor as my body starts dry-heaving again.

The notion of a peaceful night's sleep feels like a distant fantasy. Each time I lay down and close my eyes, a restless dance ensues. My muscles protest with painful cramps. Beads of sweat cascade down my body, leaving me shivering once again.

"Lean on me," Lindsay urges as she threads her arm under mine and around my back, helping me from the bed. "You need a dry T-shirt. This one is soaked." Gently, she helped me lift my arms and remove the drenched shirt. "Are you okay with sitting here while I put clean sheets on the bed?"

"You don't have to do this," I confess, my embarrassment evident in my voice as I struggle with my basic needs.

"I know," she says reassuringly, her actions speaking volumes as she wipes my face with a warm washcloth. "I want to help."

"I'd rather you didn't see me like this."

She lets out an amused huff. "Now you sound like Donnie."

"He wants to protect you from the evil in the world."

"I'm not a child," Lindsay protests as she drags the washcloth over my chest. "My boyfriend is the president of a motorcycle gang." She sticks her tongue out at me, trying to lighten the mood.

I try to laugh but end up doubled over with stomach cramps. "I'm sorry," she says, rubbing my back. "Take slow, deep breaths and relax your muscles."

It takes a few minutes for the cramping to subside. Slowly, I slacken my arms and sit back up. "How do you know what to do?"

"I'm a nurse," she admits as she helps me pull a soft T-shirt over my head.

"But you work at a convenience store?"

"I used to work at the ER at Rady Children's Hospital, but the stress got to be too much," she sighs. "Right now, I'm taking a break from it," she explains while she strips the bed. "Donnie owns the store. I'm working there a few days a week while I figure out the direction I want to take next."

"Yet you're here taking care of me while I go through withdrawal. You're an angel."

"Leo," Ramiro says my name as he shakes my shoulder gently. "You need to get up and try to eat."

"How long have I been sleeping?" I ask as I stretch my arms above my head.

"Twelve hours. Give or take a few." He turns the bedside lamp on, illuminating the room in soft lighting.

I throw my legs over the side of the bed. "Why does it feel like it was only an hour or two?"

"The past few weeks have been hard on you," he explains. "Your body's still recovering."

When Donnie said the next few days of my life would be hell, he wasn't exaggerating. Over the past two weeks, my mind and body suffered in ways I never dreamed imaginable. Sweats. Chills. Muscle cramps. Itching. The feeling of bugs crawling over every centimeter of my skin. Nausea. Vomiting.

There were countless instances when the desperation brought me to my knees, begging for more drugs. In those dark moments, the allure of staying addicted seemed preferable to enduring another agonizing second of withdrawal. In those gut-wrenching moments, Donnie's stern talks became my lifeline. He insisted I was stronger than the torment I was enduring.

"I need to ask you something." I look Ramiro in the eye, finally having the courage to ask the question that's been on my mind since the night I was rescued. "Why did Donnie step in to help me? He doesn't know me."

"That's Donnie's story to tell, not mine."

"Are you two coming?" Lindsay pops her head into my room. "The food's going to be cold."

At this precise instant, my stomach makes itself known with a growl. "What's for dinner? I'm starving."

"I'm so happy to hear that." Her face lights up. "Donnie's grilling steaks and I made baked potatoes and fresh broccoli."

"That sounds delicious." I stand and start walking toward the door. "What are we waiting for?"

Anthony

It's a busy night at Fire and Ice tonight. I look out at the club's main room from the door to the kitchen. I've been here all day putting together a new menu and ensuring the new ordering system is all in place and working correctly. Now that everything's in order, I need to find Owen and let him know I'm going home. Between all the hours I'm putting in at *Italiano Desiderio* and the hours I put in at the club's restaurant, I'm ready for an early night.

I wander through the club, stopping to say hi to a few friends before I spot him. "I'm heading out. I wanted to say goodbye before I left."

"Why don't you stick around?" Owen slides the print off of the subs who are looking to play toward me.

"I don't know." It's been over a year since Kam died. I've thought about trying to play with a new sub but haven't taken any steps to do so. In my head, I worry about what people will think. Is it too soon? Has it been too long?

"I'm not suggesting you make a lifelong commitment. Between here and your place, all you do is work. It's okay to take some time to relax and have fun," he encourages. "There are several good-looking men who haven't stopped watching you since you got here."

"Is that so?" Owen has me intrigued, and I skim the list again, paying attention only to names that are looking for a non-sexual scene. Where I'm willing to play, I'm not ready to get *that* involved. "What about this one?" I point to a name on the list. "What do you know about him?"

Owen quickly types the name into his system. "Trevor's been a submissive for ten years and is not interested in being collared. He's bi and is open to playing with one or more partners. Is looking for a sexual or non-sexual scene." He looks up at me. "And he hasn't taken his eyes off you the entire time you've been talking to me." He motions behind me with his chin.

I look over my shoulder to find a man, Trevor, I presume, watching us. My initial thought is he's incredibly handsome. Tall and well-built, not in the chiseled gym workout kind of way, but rather a man who stays fit through physical labor. He's standing with a small group of people, but he's not listening to them. Instead, his eyes are locked with mine.

"Wax play is on his green list," Owen adds, knowing I won't be able to resist.

"Can I reserve a room?" I can't believe the words that just came out of my mouth.

"Room Four is all yours." Owen grins like the Chesire Cat. "Happy playing."

It's been over a decade since I've had a first meeting with a man. My stomach is in knots as I approach the group. "Excuse me, folks." They fall silent, and all heads turn toward me. "Trevor, may I have a word with you?"

"Yes," he answers, and we step off to the side.

"Your name was on the list of submissives looking to scene tonight. Are you still open to that?"

"Yes, sir." His voice is deep and smooth.

I extend my hand to shake his. "I'm Tony."

"You obviously already know I'm Trevor," he remarks, a smile accompanying the handshake.

"Do you have experience with wax?"

"I've participated in a few scenes."

"I'd like to do a wax scene. In a private room," I hesitate before continuing, "There will be no sex. Are you good with that?"

"I'd be honored."

He follows me down the hall. With each step, the music and voices from the main room become quieter. When we reach room four, I swipe my membership card and step inside. I wait until the door clicks closed before continuing the conversation.

"You'll remain partially clothed. I prefer to keep you blindfolded during the scene," I continue in a matter-of-fact tone, ensuring there are enough barriers to prevent any emotions or feelings from creeping in. "Are you in agreement with all of that?"

"I am, Sir."

"I'd prefer you to call me Tony." Trevor's eyebrows raise slightly in confusion. "I don't want any of the labels or power dynamics. Tonight, we're just two men, equals, enjoying a relaxing scene."

"I understand, Tony." He offers me a kind smile that makes his beautiful brown eyes light up.

"Undress down to your underwear. I'll get the candles ready." This room has been designed explicitly for scenes involving wax. Owen and Star keep it stocked with all the necessary supplies. I go to the black lacquered chest of drawers and take out a new set of colored soy candles. They're not the ones I usually use, but I have experience and am comfortable using them.

"What do you do for a living? I ask and watch out of the corner of my eye as Trevor removes his dark green T-shirt, pulling it over his head and folding it neatly before setting it on the table.

"I'm an ironworker," he says as he removes his sneakers before undoing his dark denim jeans and adding them to the pile.

I set the candles on a small table next to the bed. "Do you work in the city?"

"I travel quite a bit with my job," he explains. "I've been in Manhattan the past few weeks, working at Grou—." He abruptly stops.

"You're working at Ground Zero?" I ask and notice the look of apprehension on Trevor's face, so I attempt to clear the air. "I'm sure you know I lost my partner on September 11th."

"I do, and I'm very sorry for your loss."

"Thank you." The familiar ache I feel in my heart when I talk about Kam returns. "You don't have to walk on eggshells, though. I'm okay to talk about it."

"If it's all the same, *I'd* rather not talk about it." A dark shadow crosses his face. "Being there every day is difficult. I need a break from the stress and heavy emotions."

"I can respect that. Lie down on your back." I gesture to the bed. "Let's get started on that relaxation."

While Trevor gets comfortable, I dim the lights and pull up my meditation playlist before returning to the table. "Lift your head." I slide the blindfold in place and then light the first candle.

Slowly, I allow the black wax to drip low on his abdomen, right where his muscles form a v, and dive below the waistband of his boxers. Next, I add grey, drizzling it through the black, creating a dark base.

Even though we're not going to be having sex of any kind, the scene wouldn't be complete without exploring the sensual aspects of hot wax. Taking a dark blue candle, I move higher and allow it to drip over Trevor's nipples. He inhales sharply.

I continue covering his muscular chest, creating a dark and stormy sky.

Creating art on a person is something I love to do. It's an extension of who I am, and it's been missing this past year. Although it feels good to be back in my element, something about this feels off. Kameron and I shared a special connection. We were in love. Words weren't necessary between us. His breaths naturally synched with my movements. Even blindfolded, he could sense my every step. This, tonight, feels stilted—wrong.

I struggle to not let my internal conflict affect Trevor's experience. He communicated the stress he's trying to escape, and I want to be able to give him that. I pause briefly and refocus my thoughts before continuing to work on my living canvas.

Going into this scene, I didn't have a plan for the design. I allowed the music and the mood to dictate my art. The product is a striking scene. The sky is a tumultuous mix of blues as if it's angry. Below it, blacks and greys resemble a pile of rubble—twisted steel. I'm taken back by the darkness.

"I'm going to set a candle on your chest. I need you to stay very still."

"Okay."

The candle adds the necessary light and hope to an otherwise bleak picture.

"Do you mind if I take a few pictures before I remove the wax?"

"I don't mind at all."

Grabbing my phone, I snap photos from several angles, being sure to capture every aspect of the design. "Are you ready?"

"To be honest, no," Trevor laughs softly.

After extinguishing the candle, I start lifting the wax from his torso. My hands skate across his skin, and although I notice the erection tenting his boxers, I choose to ignore it. "I think I got everything," I say as I finish wiping his chest.

"Would I be able to have a copy of the pictures?"

"Of course. What's your number? I'll text them to you." Trevor tells me his number, and I attach the photos to a message and hit send.

An awkward silence fills the room as Trevor gets dressed. This isn't like any scene I've ever done. I've broken many rules by not having a more in-depth conversation about experience and limits.

What do I do now? Typically, I'd give aftercare, but since I dismissed our roles as a Dominant and submissive, I don't think that's the proper next step. Shaking hands and parting ways doesn't seem right either.

"These are incredible," Trevor says as he scrolls through the pictures. "Thank you again, Tony. This was exactly what I needed."

"I'm glad you had a good time." I continue cleaning up the candles, still debating what my next move should be.

Trevor steps up next to me. "Can I help you with this?"

"I've got it."

"Tony." Trevor places his hand on my arm. "Please let me clean up. It's the least I can do."

I take a deep breath before stepping out of his way. "I appreciate it."

I watch as he collects the remaining candles and strips the waterproof sheet off the bed.

After he finishes sweeping up, he comes over to where I'm sitting. "I think I got it all," he says and pauses. He looks around nervously before continuing, "If that's everything, I'll just head out."

"Have a good evening." I nod and watch as he walks toward the door. An internal battle rages within me, debating whether to muster the courage to stop him. I don't want to lead him on, but I also know I shouldn't let him leave like this. I jump up just as he reaches for the handle. "Wait." He pulls his hand back and turns to face me. "Do you want to grab something to eat?"

"I'd like that a lot."

Anthony

After signing out of the club, Trevor and I stroll down the busy New York City street to a small but busy restaurant a few blocks away. I debated staying at Fire and Ice but knew everyone would be watching and wondering if something was developing between us. I didn't want to put Trevor or myself under that much pressure.

We're sat in a cozy booth. Our server comes over right away and we order our drinks. I'm perusing the menu when Trevor abruptly sets his down and admits hurriedly, "I apologize for my body's reaction at the end of the scene. I know you said nothing sexual, and I went and did that."

I set my menu down. "Please don't apologize."

His shoulders drop as he speaks. "My lack of self-control made things uncomfortable."

"I didn't see it as a lack of anything. Wax scenes are inherently sensual." I stop talking when I see the server approaching. We give our orders. I wait until we're alone before continuing, "Your arousal was natural. I wish I could've offered you more."

"I wasn't expecting more. I knew exactly—"

I hold up my hand, interrupting him. "Please let me apologize." Trevor's eyebrows draw together in confusion. "I'm an experienced Dominant, and I handled tonight entirely wrong. You deserved more—better than what I gave you."

"May I say something?" he asks, waiting for my approval. "You stated the expectations clearly, and I accepted your offer with the understanding that it wouldn't be a typical scene."

"You're being too gracious." Our food is brought to the table, pausing our conversation once again. We begin eating in silence. I don't want the rest of the evening to continue as awkward as it feels right now. Trying to lighten the mood, I say, "Tell me about yourself."

"I'm originally from upstate New York," he says, then explains that he enlisted in the Army right after high school graduation. "My plan was to be career military, but life had other ideas in mind for me, and I retired two years ago."

"May I ask why?"

"My sister, Lisa, was in the wrong place at the wrong time," he says, his voice cracking from emotion. "She was shot in a drive-by."

"I'm so sorry."

"She left behind a six-month-old baby girl, Paisley." He closes his eyes for a moment. "I was stationed in South Korea when I got the call."

Before losing Kameron, I never paid attention to or considered just how many people have suffered significant losses and are walking around with pieces of their hearts missing.

"That must've been awful."

"I've never felt so helpless." He blinks back tears. "Knowing Paisley was here alone, and I was halfway across the world." Trevor must sense my confusion because he explains further. "Paisley's father walked when he found out Lisa was pregnant. It took ten days for me to get back here. Thankfully, my SO was able to pull some strings, and Paisley was able to stay with his wife back on base until I got home."

"I'm sure that was a small relief for you."

"It was. Even though Paisley didn't know them, at least I knew she was being cared for until I could get to her."

I smile. "So, now you're raising a little girl."

"I am." Trevor beams as he grabs his phone and turns the screen toward me. "She's two and a half now."

I look at the picture of a beautiful blonde-haired, green-eyed little girl smiling at the camera, hugging a stuffed animal. "She gorgeous."

"She's become my whole world."

The longing to be a parent tugs at my heart. "I can imagine."

"It's been a huge adjustment. My job requires a lot of travel, so I had to hire a nanny I could trust to move around with us. That's who's with her tonight." He sets his phone down. "I don't go out much these days. But Andrea, Paisley's nanny, insisted I take a night to myself."

"I haven't gone out much since Kameron passed." I look up at Trevor. "But I'm glad I went to the club tonight."

We enjoy more pleasant conversation while we finish dinner. By the end of the evening, I find myself hating to see it end.

After settling our check, we go back outside. It's late, and the heavier crowds have dispersed, leaving only a few people walking about. "I had a great time tonight."

"So did I." Trevor pauses, looking uncertain. "I'm leaving to go back home in the morning. But I'll be back in the city after Christmas. I'm wondering if you'd be open to seeing each other again?" I felt nothing toward him when we were doing the scene and find I'm at a loss for a reply. "I'm sorry," he apologizes quickly. "I shouldn't have asked that. You made it clear this was a one-time thing." He tries to wave me off.

"It's okay," I assure him, placing my hand on his arm. "I have to be honest. I don't know if I'm ready for another relationship, but I'm open to keeping in touch," I respond, wondering if putting more effort into this might spark attraction. Perhaps I'm just out of practice.

"I'd like that very much." He offers me a dazzling smile.

We part ways as Trevor heads back to his hotel, and I return to my apartment. Alone.

Leopold

DINNER WAS FANTASTIC. IT MARKED THE FIRST TIME I could eat without the constant fear of vomiting. Despite not wanting to ruin the positive vibes, there's a pressing question that's been on my mind. "What happens next? I know I can't go back to Safe Haven. Donnie and Lindsay have been generous in opening their home to me," I convey my gratitude. "But I know I can't stay here forever."

"You're welcome to stay with us as long as you need," Donnie adds.

"Leo's right," Ramiro interjects, setting his fork down. "We need to have a serious conversation about where he goes from here. I tried appealing to the board at Safe Haven, but they were resistant to making an exception and letting you back before the six months are up."

"I thought that program was yours," Donnie adds, annoyed.

"It is. But we have a board of directors who oversees policies and decision-making," Ramiro explains.

"He can't go back out there alone," Lindsay says panicked.

"We're not letting him go anywhere on his own." Donnie takes her hand, placing a gentle kiss on it.

"My biggest concern is that Safe Haven's in Krew's territory. Even if he came back…" Ramiro's voice trails off.

"There's room in our building. He can stay with my guys." Donnie leans forward, resting his elbows on the table. "They'll make sure he's safe, but he'll have to stay confined to my neighborhood."

"Having your movement restricted and always feeling the need to look over your shoulder is no way to live." Ramiro sits back in his chair and sighs loudly.

"Hello." I wave my hand. "You two are talking about me like I'm not here."

"Sorry about that," Donnie apologizes with a slight shrug.

I look between the two men who are trying to decide my future right in front of me. "Don't I get a say in where I go?"

"For once, Vega's right," Donnie admits, tapping on the table.

"Can you say that again?" Ramiro holds his hand to his ear and laughs.

The banter between Ramiro and Donnie suggests they've known each other longer than the past few weeks. A subtle undercurrent suggests they might not be exactly friends.

Donnie narrows his eyes at Ramiro. "Don't push it, Vega."

"You're not going to like my suggestion, Leo." Ramiro shifts his attention to me. "I think it would be best for you to relocate."

"Leave San Diego?" My stomach sinks.

"Leave California," Ramiro says cautiously.

For a moment, I'm too stunned to speak. "And go where?"

"I reached out to some contacts I have in Manhattan," he says cautiously.

I nearly choke on a mouthful of water. "As in, New York City?"

Ramiro explains this couple runs a program similar to Safe Haven and that he's already contacted them to see if they'd be able to help. "They have an opening in one of their group apartments," he finally says.

"Group apartments?" I question, a noticeable hesitation creeping into my voice. "What does that mean?"

"Instead of having one building where you get a room, they own several properties around the city. You'll share an apartment with a few roommates who are also in the program," Ramiro explains, with a measured tone indicating thoughtful consideration. "They offer significantly discounted rent to the young people in their program."

I listen carefully to what he's saying. "There are four people in an apartment, and there are no co-ed living spaces," he adds. "They also have connections with employers in the city who prioritize giving people in their program a first chance at any job openings."

I was born and raised in Rolling Hills. It was all I knew until my parents dumped me at Walking in the Light. San Diego took a lot of getting used to, but at least I was in California. I was starting to put roots down for myself.

Now, because of the mess I made getting involved with Krew, I'm faced with leaving everyone and everything I know to start over on the East Coast. I want to be mad. To scream and fight. Heck, I'll even beg. How dare they tell me I have to leave? I sigh in resignation, knowing there's nothing I can do. There's no one to blame for this. No one other than myself.

"Oh," I say quietly.

Donnie eyes me carefully before saying, "You don't have to decide anything tonight. Let's get you back on your feet before you make any major life plans."

Ramiro's phone chimes. He checks it before saying, "It's my wife. I promised her I'd be home tonight." He shifts his focus to me. "As long as you're comfortable here without me."

"Of course," I smile, hoping to hide the tumultuousness churning just below the surface. Ramiro's already given up enough for me. I can't ask him to do anything more.

"Can I talk to you about something before you leave?" Lindsay asks Ramiro.

"Sure," He gets to his feet. Giving me a final glance, he says, "I'll give you a call tomorrow."

I nod and watch as Linsday walks outside with him, leaving Donnie and me alone in the house.

"You okay?" he asks, running his hand over his face. "That was a shit ton of information to swallow."

Am I okay? I'm numb. It's like I'm watching a movie about someone else's life. Except it's not a movie. It's real life, and I'm the star. "I guess." I shrug. "It's not like I have any choice."

"I'll admit, your options are limited, but you always have a choice." He motions toward the door. "If you don't like what Vega's suggesting, we'll figure out something better."

I gather the dinner plates and bring them to the sink. "His offer is very generous." I turn around and force a smile. "It's a chance to start over." Donnie crosses his arms over his. "Have you ever been to New York?" I ask him.

"Me? No." He shakes his head.

"I'll be sure to let you know what it's like there."

Leopold

I HAD HOPED FOR MORE TIME, BUT ONCE RAMIRO MADE the call, I was given no more than two weeks to get to New York and complete the intake into the program before I'd lose my place. Getting me ready for my cross-country move has been the top priority.

None of Krew's *clients* used protection, so one of the many things on my to-do list was blood work to make sure I was clean. Donnie and Lindsay brought me earlier this week. The results came back yesterday. I got lucky, and I'm okay.

Ramiro has been more than generous, ensuring that not only do I have a safe place to go but that I have clothes to go with. He and his wife purchased me a small wardrobe of clothes to get me started. They also included a winter coat and boots—clothing items I've never owned or considered needing. They also purchased me a bus ticket, which was the last thing I needed to leave for New York later tonight.

I'm stuffing my clothes into my new black duffel bag when Donnie appears in my doorway. "Do you mind if I come in?" he asks.

"Of course not."

He enters the room and takes a seat on the chair, the same one that he and Ramiro occupied for countless hours while the effects of the drugs leaving my body attempted to overwhelm me.

I stop what I'm doing and turn to him. "There's something I've been wondering about."

"Okay," he says and sits back, his legs spread.

"How do you and Ramiro know each other?"

His eyes take on a far-away look before he says, "I didn't come from upstanding people. The sperm donor, whoever he was, didn't stick around. The woman who gave birth to me, well, that's the only credit I can give her. Hell, most days, I wished she'd aborted me. In many ways, it would've been kinder." I pull my legs onto the bed while I listen to his story.

"My mother was a drug-addicted whore who had a revolving door of men in her bed. Anything to get her next fix," he adds. "It was a wonder I survived my early childhood years. By the time I was thirteen, she was rarely around anymore," he says. "Child Welfare Services showed up one day and took me away. They relocated me to an upscale neighborhood with a two-parent family and a new *brother* that was my age."

"Ramiro," I say quietly, and Donnie nods.

"Within an hour of my arrival, his parents brought me for a haircut and purchased a new wardrobe so I'd fit in with their fancy friends. Couldn't have the foster child from the city making them look bad," he says with a touch of sarcasm." Before I knew it, we were in front of a judge, and they were adopting me." I try hard not to react to his bombshell. Donnie crosses his legs before continuing. "I didn't harbor any notions about going back to my biological mother, but I also didn't want to be adopted—not that anyone asked my opinion. I hated them," he states matter-of-factly. "I made it my life's mission to make their lives hell. A punishment for adopting me."

Donnie continues, "I'd sneak out at night looking for trouble. The funny thing is when you're looking for it, you'll always find it. I started stealing and running drugs. I was sloppy, though, and ended up in juvie." He chuckles. "They were there to bail me out and brought me back home to love me through it. I didn't want to be loved, though. So, I scaled up my behaviors at home and school—when I bothered to show up. Things went downhill fast when they found a gun in my room."

"Why did you have a gun?" I ask, my chin resting on my hands.

"I joined a gang," he says matter-of-factly. "Alfonso, Ramiro's father, lost his shit on me. He'd brought in the wooden paddle, but before he could use it, Ramiro started screaming in the other room. Ella, his mother, had collapsed. They brought her to the emergency room and found out she had a heart attack. The doctors denied that stress had anything to do with it, but I knew." He runs his fingers through his hair. "Alfonso didn't leave her side while she was recovering in the hospital. That's when Vega and I had a fight."

"A physical fight?" I ask, unable to picture Ramiro being violent with anyone.

"Yes. It wasn't much of one, though. Vega's strong suit is not fighting," He grins. "I landed a few hits and broke his nose. He was lying on the floor, curled in a ball. I thought it was over and stepped over him to walk away. Then, I heard the safety of my gun click off. I spun around and found him pointing it at my head."

I'm invested in his story and inquire, "How did he get your gun?"

"Like I said, I was sloppy. I left it out in my room. Vega was extremely protective of his mother, and he became desperate. He grabbed the gun and threatened to kill me if I didn't agree to leave and never come back." My mouth hangs open in shock, unable to picture Ramiro doing something so extreme. "He didn't have to ask me twice. Not because I was afraid of him, but because I didn't want to be there anyway."

"How old were you?"

"It was my sixteenth birthday. But with everything going on, no one remembered," Donnie admits. For the briefest of seconds, I see the look of disappointment on his face, but he quickly schools his features. "I grabbed my bag and a few pieces of my shit and never looked back."

"I can't believe he was that cruel," I mumbled, disappointed in the man I look up to as a mentor—a father figure.

"Vega wasn't cruel. He did what he had to do to protect his parents," he says without hesitation. "I didn't see or hear from him again for many years. Not until Ella was dying. Vega came looking for me because her last wish was to have her two boys back together again."

"How did he know where to find you?"

"Vega was here in San Diego. He opened Safe Haven a few months prior, and I was making a name for myself in other circles. One afternoon, he showed up on my corner and told me I had to go with him." He laughs at the memory. "You had to see his face with more than one weapon pointed at him."

I can't help the quiet chuckle that escapes, picturing Ramiro trying to force Donnie to do anything. "Did you go with him?"

"It was the least I could do for all the shit I put them through. They were good people who really cared about me, and I was a fucking punk who tried to derail their lives." He shifts uncomfortably in his seat. "We got to the hospice with enough time to promise her that Vega and I would make amends and would take care of each other. Alfonso passed away a year before, and Vega had no other family. I couldn't say no to a dying woman, so I agreed," he says softly.

"Even though we don't have the best relationship, I understand he's a good guy who's trying to make a difference." He shrugs. "Maybe that was part of the problem all along. I knew he was a much better person than I'd ever be."

"I don't think that's true," I interrupt. "Anyone who takes in a stranger and nurses them through withdrawal can't possibly be a bad person."

"We're going to have to agree to disagree, kid." Donnie smiles. "Anyway, I came in here to give you this." He reaches into his pocket and pulls out a wad of folded cash.

My eyes grow wide. "I can't take that."

"I might not have ever visited the place, but I can tell you that New York's expensive. You'll need some cash until you get on your feet." He pushes the money into my hand.

"I don't know how I can ever repay you for everything you've done for me." I'm beginning to get emotional, and my voice cracks.

Donnie stands, and I swear I see him quickly wipe under his eye. "You're a good kid, Leo. Go to New York and do something great with your life. Make a difference."

He doesn't wait for my reply before walking out of the room. I sit stunned not only at the history between Donnie and Ramiro but also at the two thousand dollars in cash he left me with.

Before I know it, Ramiro arrives to bring me to the bus station.

Lindsay sobs as I hug her goodbye. Donnie stands off to the side, his arms tightly crossed over his chest. Catching his eye, he nods subtly, prompting me to respond with a warm, understanding smile, conveying my gratitude for everything he's done for me.

"Ready to go?"

I can't hold back my tears any longer, and I fear if I don't leave now, I'll change my mind, so I hurry out the door without looking back.

With a heavy heart, I am closing the book on the only life I've ever known. A surge of fear accompanies a small but tangible excitement as I set my sights on the uncertain path that lies ahead for me in the bustling landscape of the Big Apple.

Anthony

Italiano Desiderio has quickly become *the* place to eat in lower Manhattan. Since our opening, we've hosted more stars than I can count. Our reservations are booked out for the next six months. I never imagined my restaurant would reach this level of success ever, let alone in its first year.

The reality of owning a restaurant is far from glamorous. It's a continuous effort. Managing staff to meet a standard I can be proud of requires long hours and dedication. Tonight was exceptionally busy, so I joined my kitchen staff to stay on top of orders. The experience was both invigorating and exhausting, capturing the essence of the demanding yet fulfilling nature of the job.

The employees left over an hour ago. I stayed to catch up on some paperwork. No longer able to focus, I decide to call it a night. After doing a final walk-through, I switch off the lights and am about to lock up when my phone rings. I glance down, a smile coming to my face when I see it's Jennifer.

"Hello."

A sob-filled voice responds, "It's me."

My pulse shoots up instantly. "What's wrong?"

"I just got a call. My mom fell again," she says and stops to blow her nose. "Her neighbor hadn't seen her in a few days and tried to call her. When Mom's answering machine kept picking up, she decided to go over. She knocked, but Mom didn't come to the door."

Jennifer's mom lives alone in a two-story home entirely too big and dangerous for an eighty-three-year-old woman. She's had several falls in the past six months. Jenn's begged her to either move to the city with her or into an assisted living facility, but her mother refused. As a compromise, Jennifer hired home health aides, but her mother is challenging to deal with, and they all quit after a few weeks. She's been at her wit's end as to what to do.

"Is she okay?"

"I don't know." She starts crying again. "Apparently, she called 911. The police and fire department came and had to break a window to get into the house. They're on the way to the emergency room now."

"What can I do?"

"I know it's late, but can you come here?" she asks.

"I'm getting on the train now. I'll be there as soon as I can."

I arrive at her house about twenty minutes later. When I walk in, she's on the phone with the hospital.

"How long will she be in the hospital?" She asks. "Yes, I understand. Thank you, doctor."

Jen sets the phone on her kitchen counter and drops her head into her hands.

"What did they say?" I ask, putting my arm around her for support.

"Mom fell down the stairs. From the looks of it, she was there for a few days. They have her on fluids for dehydration. She had five stitches for a gash on her forehead, and she fractured her ankle. Thankfully, there are no internal injuries." She drops onto a stool at the island in her kitchen. "I can't keep doing this, Tony. Without being there full-time, I can't keep her safe."

Jenn and I have become close friends over the past few years. We've been there for one another as we've healed from our losses. I've been privileged to be a part of her girls' lives and have watched them grow. I've also had a front-row seat as Jennifer struggled with how to deal with her ailing mother's health.

Over the past year, she's traveled back and forth as much as possible. The girls and she spent the summer in Pennsylvania. But now that Anna's starting kindergarten, she can't pick up and go whenever her mom needs something. It's added a significant amount of stress to her already burdened shoulders.

"After Mom's last accident, I met with a realtor," she admits, crestfallen. "I'm sorry. I should've told you sooner."

I try to mask my surprise. "You don't owe me any explanations."

"I know, but we're friends," she says, wiping her eyes. "Selling this house breaks my heart. Jeff and I started our family here. It's the only place I feel close to him. At the same time, my mother needs me."

"You'll take Jeff with you wherever you go," I say and take her hands. "As much as I'll hate your leaving, you need to do what's best for you and the girls."

"There's been a lot of interest in the property already. It won't take long for it to sell," she adds, and again, I'm shocked at how much effort she's already put into moving. Jennifer looks down at where our hands are joined before continuing, "It's going to be so hard on the girls. Everything they know is here."

"It'll be an adjustment, but kids are resilient." I offer her a reassuring smile. "They'll be okay."

She picks up her phone and opens a web browser. "I have to find plane tickets. The doctor said she'll be in the hospital for a few days, but I want to get there as soon as possible."

Knowing Jennifer and the girls are leaving for good is an emotional blow I wasn't expecting. But I can't wallow in self-pity. She's struggling and needs me to be strong for her. "What can I do to help?"

"Can you stay the night and help me explain everything to the girls in the morning?"

"Of course."

Anna and Chloe are up with the sun and excited to go on an airplane to visit their Nana. Jennifer tries to explain that they'll be moving to Pennsylvania. However, the girls are still young, and I don't think they completely grasped the concept.

Jenn and I spent the better part of the day packing suitcases they'll take on their flight and packing a few boxes filled with things she and the girls will need right away that I'll take to the shipping center.

The adults are exhausted when we're finally piling into our Uber on the way to JFK. Jenn stares out the window, swiping at her eyes. I attempt to keep the girls distracted, giving her some time to sit with her emotions. It also keeps my mind off the fact that I'll miss them all terribly.

"The realtor said we can handle everything online," Jenn says, pulling herself together as the airport comes into view. "I'll have to hire a moving company to pack the house and get our stuff to Clearfield."

"You know I'll be here to help with whatever I can," I say as I grab the suitcases out of the trunk.

"You have enough on your plate with the restaurant." She clicks the handle into the up position on a Disney princess suitcase. "Anna, I need you to take this."

"Are you coming too?" Chloe asks, looking up at me with her big blue eyes.

And I thought my heart couldn't break anymore. "No, Chloe Bear." I scoop her into my arms. "Uncle Tony has to stay here."

"Will you come visit us?" Anna asks, pushing out her bottom lip.

"Of course I will." I grab Chloe's bag with my free hand. "Come on. If we don't get moving, you'll miss your flight."

We keep Anna between us as she wheels her pink princess

suitcase through the busy airport. Jennifer talks about everything and nothing, something she does when she's nervous, until we stop at the security checkpoint. Jennifer takes Chloe's hand when I set her down.

"I guess this is where we say goodbye," Jennifer says with tears in her eyes.

"How about we say see you later instead?" I suggest, unable to say goodbye.

"I like that better." She manages to force a smile. "Give Uncle Tony hugs."

Getting down to Anna's level, she wraps her tiny arms around my neck. "Will you come to see us soon?" she asks, her bottom lip quivering.

"As soon as I can," I say and kiss her forehead.

I move to Chloe, who gives me a big kiss on my cheek. "I love you, Uncle Tony," she says, looking back at me and waving from the other side of the checkpoint.

I wait until they're out of sight before returning to the waiting Uber.

Loneliness overwhelms me as I sit in the back of the much quieter car. I drop my head onto the seat behind me. I'm tired of saying goodbye.

When will the universe bring someone into my life and, this time, allow them to become a permanent part of my story?

Anthony

I'm awaiting my midweek food delivery at *Italiano Desiderio*. Unfortunately, winter limits my ability to cultivate more than a few herbs inside the restaurant. Thankfully, one of the perks of living in Manhattan is the availability of high-quality fresh groceries.

A gust of cold air blows through the restaurant when the front door opens. The delivery guy is precariously balancing several boxes.

"Let me give you a hand with those." I hurry over and grab the top box.

"Thanks," he says from buried beneath his scarf. "It's freezing out there."

"It's certainly a chilly one today." I set the box down and follow him outside to grab another one. It's only mid-November, and we're already getting a taste of what winter will bring. "You're not Joey," I remark. "Are you new?"

"Yes and no," he says, setting the last box on the stainless-steel kitchen counter. After peeling his scarf open, he says while removing his gloves, "I usually work in the stock room, but Joey quit without notice, so I'm doing the deliveries today."

"I'm Tony." I extend my hand, the warmth of the room contrasting with the cool touch of my skin.

"Leopold." He smiles, the corners of his lips curving with an inviting charm as he shakes my hand.

At that moment, an instant attraction sparks within me, a magnetic pull that lingers in the air, though I'm unsure if he senses it, too.

With a tactful retreat of my hand, I offer, "It's nice to meet you, Leopold." I test the feel of his name on my lips. "Do you have time for a quick coffee? It'll warm you up before you have to go back out," I say, glancing outside at the gentle snow that's begun falling.

A moment of hesitation flickers across his face as he bites his lower lip before answering, "Sure. That'd be great."

"Grab a seat while I go get it."

While I busy myself making two cups of espresso, I can't help watching as Leopold unzips his dark green puffy jacket, draping it over the back of the chair. Then, he removes his beanie and shakes out his shoulder-length wavy blond hair. He's an attractive young man. Note the *young* Anthony and quit staring at the guy. I mentally chastise myself.

However, I can't shake the overwhelming desire to do something nice for him—to care for him. Looking around, I spot the cannoli I just finished filling. With the dessert in one hand and the espresso in the other, I bring them to where he's sitting.

When he spots the sweet treat, his ice-blue eyes light up. "Thanks," he says and doesn't waste a second picking up the pastry and taking a bite. His eyes close as he moans, and God help me. The sound stirs something in me that hasn't felt alive in a very long time. "Mmm. This tastes like heaven."

A smile plays on my lips as I say, "I'm glad you like it."

"Like it?" He meets my gaze. "I love it." His tongue licks at some stray powdered sugar from his lower lip, and I force myself to look away. "Are you the manager here?" he asks.

"I'm a little of everything," I laugh softly. "This is my place."

"Oh wow. That's really awesome." His voice is filled with awe. "I can't imagine being able to own my own business," he says as he continues eating.

Some days, I still can't believe that not only is this place mine, but it's also hugely successful. "I did my fair share of working for other people. This was a long time in the making," I say as I grab my cup off the bar and return to the table. "If having your own business is your dream, I have no doubt you'll achieve it."

"I'll have to take your word on that." He wipes his mouth and pushes the chair back to stand. "I should be getting back. Where can I put these?"

"Leave them there. I'll take care of it."

"Thanks for the snack," he says as he hurries to grab his coat.

I can't help but chuckle watching this kid bundle up like we're in the Arctic. "Not a fan of the cold?"

"I wasn't made for winter," he says as he tucks his blond locks back into his hat. "I much prefer the heat and sun."

"Where are you from, Leopold?"

"You can call me Leo," he says, gracing me with a smile. "I'm from California."

"You're a long way from home."

"Tell me about it," he mumbles.

Something about Leo has me scrambling to find a way to keep him here longer. "What brought you to the East Coast?"

He wraps his scarf over his face before responding, "Looking to try something new. I guess." He shrugs. "Can you sign this for me?"

"Sure." I grab a pen from the hostess station and scribble my name on the bottom.

He pulls them apart and hands me the top copy. "Thanks again for the coffee and snack."

"Anytime."

Leo walks out of my restaurant, looking like the weight of the world is on his shoulders, and I'm left with a longing to fix it all for him.

Leopold

GETTING OUT OF THE STOCKROOM TO MAKE EACH DAY'S deliveries is the most exciting thing that's happened in my otherwise dull and lonely life since I've been in New York City.

Ramiro's friends claimed their program was similar to Safe Haven, but that couldn't be further from the truth. Safe Haven offered so much more than just a roof over my head. Ramiro and the rest of the staff were invested in helping us make something more of ourselves. We were assigned the responsibility of earning our GEDs and were then encouraged to apply for post-secondary education. Job training and assistance securing employment were provided so we could each experience the pride and satisfaction of earning a paycheck.

The residential side of the program offered support by teaching us things like how to cook and do laundry—skills most people take for granted but that many of us were never taught. I didn't realize how good things were there until it was too late.

This program, and I use the word program loosely, is no more than subsidized housing and a packet of papers with a list of places to apply for a job. The vast majority of the businesses listed were no longer operating, which made finding a job challenging.

The apartment is a barely habitable space I share with three other men. We're crammed into one bathroom and two bedrooms. I'm lighter than my roommate, so I got lucky and was assigned the top bunk.

My roommates had lived together for several months before I arrived and were already tight with each other. They have little interest in doing anything other than playing video games or trading stories of the women they're sleeping with. Once they found out I was gay, something that only took about thirty seconds, they'd made up their minds to not include me in anything. When the weather's nice, I try to spend as little time there as possible.

I'm exceedingly thankful for the extra cash Donnie gave me before I left San Diego. He wasn't kidding when he said things were expensive here. The job at the market only pays minimum wage. It's about the best a kid with no high school diploma or GED can expect. My paycheck, combined with the money from Donnie, barely covers my share of the rent and utilities, leaving little extra to buy my own groceries—which the other guys always manage to eat. I'd love to move out, but I'm barely affording this dump with three roommates. There's no way I'd be able to afford anything else.

It's just my luck that my promotion comes during winter when the sun teases from the sky, giving the allure of warmth, but it's actually frigid. The cold air whips off the harbor as I load the boxes into the back of the taxi. Since Joey, the regular delivery guy, left my boss in a lurch, he's desperate today and is paying my taxi fare.

"Are you in there, Leopold?" Jerry, my boss, asks, looking closer at me.

"It's freezing out here." I pull my hat down further.

Jerry laughs. "It's only November. What are you going to do when it really gets cold?"

"I might not come back out until Spring." I grin, although he can't see it beneath my heavy scarf.

Although my job doesn't pay much, my boss is terrific. Jerry's had his market for over forty years. He and his late wife have been very good to me since I came here. They never had children, so they kinda took me under their wing. Now that Esther's gone, Jerry's my only friend in this otherwise lonely and unfamiliar city.

"Here's your inventory slip." Jerry hands me a handwritten invoice. Even though most of the other employees keep telling him he needs to upgrade to a computer system, he refuses. They poke fun at him for being a dinosaur, but I find it endearing. "Be sure to give this to whoever receives the order. They need to sign here." He shows me with a shaky hand. "Give them the white paper and bring the pink one back to the store."

"That's easy enough."

"You're a good kid, Leopold." He squeezes my shoulder.

Jerry watches while I continue loading boxes into the trunk of the car. "Go on back inside," I say, but he waves me off. "You're going to get sick out here with no coat." I shake my head at his sheer stubbornness. It isn't until I'm sliding into the back seat of the yellow cab that Jerry finally goes back inside.

Twenty minutes later, the cabby is screeching to a stop outside *Italiano Desiderio.*

"Here goes nothing," I say, earning a curious glance from the driver. "As soon as I unload, you can go." It might be cold, but I don't want Jerry to have to pay for my ride back to the shop. It's only a little over a mile. I can walk.

Grabbing two boxes from the opened trunk, I balance them on one arm and reach to open the door.

"Let me give you a hand with those." I hear the voice but don't see a face until he takes the top box.

"Thanks," I say, thankful my face is hidden beneath the scarf. Otherwise, he might've noticed my mouth hanging open. This man is older, but he's seriously gorgeous. He stands shorter than me by about five or six inches. But it's his eyes that strike me most —they're dark and incredibly kind. I try not to stare but fail miserably.

"Thanks. It's freezing out there," I add, a chill running

through me, but I'm unsure if it's from the cold air or the man standing next to me.

"It's certainly a chilly one today," he says before following me back outside to grab the rest of the boxes.

What's with these New Yorkers going out in this weather without a coat on? They're all crazy.

"You're not Joey," he says while I'm reaching into the trunk. "Are you new?"

"Yes and no," I reply, hastily placing the last and heaviest box on one of the counters in the restaurant's kitchen. I remove my gloves, tucking them into my coat pocket, and loosen my scarf. "I usually work in the stock room, but Joey quit without notice, so I'm doing the deliveries today."

"I'm Tony," he introduces himself, extending a hand.

"Leopold," I breathe, feeling a magnetic pull as our hands connect, a subtle yet electric current passing between us.

"It's nice to meet you, Leopold." The look on his face does funny things to my insides. "Do you have time for a quick coffee? It'll warm you up before you have to go back out there."

I start to open my mouth to respond but quickly close it. I promised myself not to be as naive or foolish as I've been in the past. To be more cautious with those who show kindness. Then, I stop myself. This guy isn't asking me to marry him. He's simply being friendly and offering me coffee because it's cold out. I take a deep breath and try to relax. "Sure. That'd be great."

"Grab a seat while I go get it," he says, disappearing into the kitchen.

I remove my jacket and put it over the back of the dark wood chair. Then, I pull off my hat and gently shake out my hair before sitting down. While I wait, I look around and take in the restaurant. It looks like a scene straight out of Italy.

A few minutes later, Tony comes out of the kitchen with a plate in one hand and a small glass mug in the other. He sets the dish in front of me, and my mouth waters. Although I've been careful to live as frugally as possible, going without many creature comforts, the money Donnie gave me is almost gone. I had a leftover slice of pizza for breakfast but haven't eaten since, so this is a welcome surprise. "Thanks," I say and sink my teeth into the cannoli. I'm not an expert, but I'm confident this is freshly made. My eyes close. "Mmm. This tastes like heaven."

"I'm glad you like it." he smiles.

"Like it." My eyes meet his. "I love it." I take another bite and lick the powdered sugar off my bottom lip. "Are you the manager here?"

"I'm a little of everything." He laughs softly. "This is my place."

"Oh wow. That's really awesome. I can't imagine being able to own my own business." I'm closing in on twenty years old, and I don't even have a high school diploma. I was lucky Jerry took a chance and hired me. Otherwise, I don't know where I'd be right now. Something like being a business owner is out of the question for a loser like me.

"I did my fair share of working for other people. This was a long time in the making." My eyes are drawn to the way his muscles flex as he walks across the room to get his coffee cup. I look away quickly when he turns back around. He takes a drink of his coffee. "If having your own business is your dream, I have no doubt you'll achieve it."

"I'll have to take your word on that." I finish my coffee and get to my feet. "Where can I put these?"

"Leave them there. I'll take care of it."

"Thanks for the snack." I slide my arms back into my coat, not relishing the thought of going back out into the snow.

"Not a fan of the cold?" Tony asks with a smile on his face.

"I wasn't made for winter," I say as I gather my hair and put it inside my hat. "I much prefer the heat and sun."

"Where are you from, Leopold?"

The sound of my name coming from his lips has the power to make me melt. I have to put a stop to any of those thoughts. "You can call me Leo," I say and smile, not wanting to sound rude. "I'm from California."

"You're a long way from home."

Home. Do I even know what that word means anymore? I can't remember the last time I felt as if I was home. "Tell me about it," I mutter.

"What brought you to the East Coast?"

Although his question sounds like he's genuinely curious, I'm not sure how to answer it. He's a complete stranger, just trying to be friendly and make small talk. He doesn't want to hear about what a screw up I am and that I had to come here to seek safety. I buy myself a few seconds by wrapping my scarf around my neck. "Looking to try something new. I guess." I reach into my pocket to get my gloves and feel the invoice. I can't believe I almost forgot it. "Can you sign this for me?" I hold out the papers.

"Sure." He steps over to the hosting station and grabs a pen. He signs his name and hands the paper back to me.

Pulling them apart, I hand him the white copy and put the pink one in my pocket. "Thanks again for the coffee and snack," I say as I put my gloves on.

"Anytime."

With that, I pull open the door and step back into the cold.

Leopold

W‍HEN I LEFT THE SHOP TO DO A DELIVERY, I WAS NOT expecting to find myself face-to-face with Tony—the most beautiful, soft-spoken man I'd ever laid eyes on. Hurrying to the end of the block and rounding the corner, I press my back against the brick building, feeling the cold permeate my coat. My unexpected reaction to Tony catches me off guard. His presence filled the room, yet he was soft-spoken. Despite my jaded perspective on life, he radiated not only positivity but also encouragement.

I've learned the hard way to be wary of strangers, yet I felt an inexplicable sense of safety in his presence. I didn't want to leave, yet a part of me wanted to run. I'm left grappling with conflicting emotions, unsure what to make of the puzzling encounter.

"It doesn't matter," I say, pushing off the wall. "It's not like I'll ever see him again." There's no way Jerry will keep paying my taxi fare when he owns a delivery truck and can hire someone who can drive it, and I can't afford to eat in a place like that.

My walk is brisk because of the temperature and my desire to return to the shop. Jerry didn't give me a timeframe to be back. However, I'm still on the clock and feel a sense of responsibility to get right back to work.

"How did that go?" Jerry asks as soon as I walk through the door.

"I think it went well." I reach into my pocket. "Here's your invoice."

Jerry inspects the document. "The in-house orders are packed and ready for you."

"Really?" I ask, surprised.

He looks at me curiously. "I told you that you were promoted to delivery."

"Yes, but I didn't think you meant permanently." I shift uncomfortably. "I don't drive."

"That's easily remedied." He walks behind the counter and pulls out a booklet. "Here."

I take the offered item and look at it. It's a study guide for the driver's exam. I look around to make sure no one is listening and then say quietly, "Even if I pass, I can't afford a car."

"You will pass," he says confidently. "And I have a car. It's old, but you can learn with it. I'll pay for driving instruction lessons."

"That's a very generous offer," I say, trying to give him the booklet back. "But I can't let you do that."

"Let me?" Jerry chuckles and shakes his head. "As your boss, it's my responsibility to provide you with training to do your job, and deliveries are now part of that job. You need to learn to drive to do it. So, as your employer, I'll ensure you get the training to do so."

"Thank you." His generosity nearly overwhelms me. "You're amazing, Jerry."

"Don't say that too loudly. I don't want anyone around here thinking I've gone soft." He gives me his signature wink. "The boxes are loaded on the dolly in the back. You missed your lunch, so I left a sandwich and drink back there for you, too."

"Actually, I had a bite to eat at the restaurant."

"Then you met Tony." He grins.

"I did," I admit, my stomach doing excited flips as the image of the attractive man crosses my mind.

"I've known him for years. He's a good man."

Needing to change the subject, I ask, "Is it okay if I bring the sandwich home for dinner?"

"Of course, it's yours, son."

Son. When I first walked in here, I was a stranger to this man. Yet Jerry's always treated me like family. On more than one occasion, he told me he felt like I was the son he never had. He would've made a wonderful father.

I'm thankful for his presence in my life, but at the same time, it hurts. Why doesn't my father care about me? Once he realized I wasn't his idea of the *perfect son,* it was so easy for him to get rid of me.

I'll never forget the look on his face when he left me at Walking in the Light. It was the first time I experienced pure hatred. What made it cut especially deep was that it was from one of the people who was supposed to love me unconditionally.

Then there's Jerry. He's older than my own father. He could probably be my grandfather. His generation wasn't raised knowing what it meant to be gay. If someone had a sexual orientation outside of the societal norms, they had to keep it hidden. Yet somehow, he recognized I was gay and accepted me—no questions asked.

I beam with pride at being called this man's son. "I'll get right on those deliveries."

Making today's deliveries was so much fun. I loved every second of meeting and talking to so many people. But it's left me exhausted. After a quick shower, I eat the ham and cheese sandwich from Jerry and collapse into bed.

Restlessness consumes me throughout the night as I dream about a strikingly handsome man. His olive skin glows with an inviting warmth, and his eyes, a kind and gentle chocolate brown, linger in my thoughts.

Anthony

❦

Sleep was elusive as I tossed and turned all night, consumed by worry about the upcoming court appearance in the morning. Finishing my shower, the sound of my phone ringing echoes from the bed. With a towel hastily wrapped around my waist, I rush to answer it, half-expecting the district attorney on the line. To my surprise, Jennifer's name illuminates the screen. I'm sure she's calling to offer me her support.

"Good morning." My effort to sound cheery falls short.

"I'm sorry to call so early," she says, her voice hoarse.

"Are you sick?"

"It's my mom," she says, barely above a whisper. "She's gone, Tony."

My heart shatters. "Oh my God, Jennifer. What happened?"

"I don't know. I came downstairs to start breakfast before I had to wake the girls up for school. Mom usually gets up as soon as she smells the coffee," Jenn pauses to catch her breath. "She's been slowing down lately, and I assumed she slept in. I was glad because I've been telling her she doesn't need to get up and help me."

"I knew. I don't know how I knew. I just did." She cries softly on the other end. "I waited until the bus came for the girls before

I went in. She looked so peaceful." Her voice carries a haunted tone."Sweetheart, I'm so sorry." I wipe the tears from my own face. My instincts urge me to pack a bag and get on the next flight to Pennsylvania, but I can't. "I have to be in court," I murmur.

"I know. I wish you didn't have to be," she says quietly. "I had at least talk to you."

Putting her on speaker, I dry off and dress in my suit and tie. The past few weeks leading up to the trial have involved extensive conversations with the district attorney. While she isn't certain I'll be called to the stand, I must be present in court, just in case.

Two of the men involved opted for plea deals, avoiding a trial. The current trial pertains to the third person involved, the minor —the one I captured in a picture, the one who threw a brick upon seeing me. Considering his past encounters with the law and the nature of his actions, the district attorney's office refrained from offering him a deal.

"My phone will be silenced, but if you need me, text or leave a voicemail. I'll check it as often as I can."

"I don't know how to tell the girls."

"Will Brian be there with you?"

Jennifer was apprehensive about moving back home. It had been a long time since she'd lived in a rural area, and other than visits, the girls only knew city life. Fortunately, Jenn reconnected with her childhood friends, who loved on her and the girls and helped them adjust to their new lives.

Despite being a full-time caregiver for her mother, Jennifer has found time to volunteer for the PTA and establish herself within the small community. Anna and Chloe are also thriving. Both girls are developing friendships, engaging in playdates, and excelling in school this year. They tell me all about it on our weekly video calls. Shortly after Christmas last year, Jennifer unexpectedly crossed paths

with her high school boyfriend, Brian. Brian, who never married, remained in Clearfield and took over the family farm. Unaware of her return, they began talking, and just like a Hallmark movie, the feelings they shared in their youth resurfaced. I met him the last time I went out to visit Jennifer. I was feeling skeptical and overprotective, but it only took minutes to see how much he adored her and the girls.

Anna has formed a strong bond with him, which was beautiful to witness, especially after how much she struggled with losing her father. Clad in her overalls, plaid shirt, and boots to match Brian's, she helps him feed the animals and get the eggs from the chickens. As much as I miss them, there's comfort in seeing all three of them so happy.

"Yes. Brian came over as soon as I called him," she explains. "He just ran out to grab a few groceries while I get the house ready. Some of my extended family is on their way. They'll be here tonight."

"I'm sure he'll help you when it's time to talk to them."

"What if this sets Anna back? I don't think I can stand to see her scared and crying all the time again. Not after how far she's come," Jenn says, her words hurried.

"She's older and can understand things better now." I do my best to reassure her, but this is uncharted territory for me. "She's going to be sad, but Anna's strong. I have no doubt she'll be okay."

We continue our conversation for a few more minutes before I reluctantly have to hang up. I'm late leaving the house and will have to hustle to get to the courthouse on time.

Who would've thought sitting all day listening to lawyers questioning experts and witnesses would be so exhausting? The prosecution wrapped up their case yesterday. Today, the defense gave their closing arguments. Thankfully, it was a short day.

I'm taking advantage of having the afternoon free and decide to stop by Fire and Ice. The club isn't open to the public right now, but I'm sure Owen or Star will be there, and right now, I could use some company.

The lights are on inside, but I don't immediately see anyone.

"I thought I heard someone come in," Owen says as he walks out of the café.

"Court let out early, and I wasn't ready to go home."

"I'm glad you came here," he says, motioning toward the kitchen. "I was just getting ready to make myself something to eat. Can I make you a plate too?"

"I can do it."

Owen holds up his hand. "Nope. Today, I'm doing the cooking."

"That would be great."

After Owen disappears in the kitchen, I check out the setups on the stages. This weekend, Fire and Ice is hosting three Dominants, Kiernan, Briar, and Charlie, from a club in the Hamptons, who will be teaching some classes and conducting demonstrations for our members.

The first stage is set up to look like a tiny apartment. There's a loveseat, a part of a kitchen countertop, and a door. Laid out on a table is a mix of spanking and sensory implements. There's a hairbrush, a feather duster, a wooden spoon, a silicone basting brush, and a silk scarf. Kiernan is known for his out-of-the-box demonstrations that show how easily BDSM can be practiced using household things rather than pricey kink-specific items.

On the middle stage is a more clinical-looking setting, complete with a violet wand, butt plugs, cock rings, nipple clamps, and an electro-Wartenberg Wheel. Charlie's clearly teaching a class on electro-play. I've sat in on their classes in the past and know they are a very experienced Dominant and a fascinating instructor. I'm sure their class will be a huge hit.

The last stage is set up for Briar to do a presentation on Disabilities and Kink. She's not only an experienced Domme, but she also holds a Doctorate in Human Sexuality. Briar's a beautiful soul who's passionate about ensuring everyone who wishes to live the BDSM lifestyle is able to find a way that works for them and their partner. I'm skimming through her class notes when I hear footsteps behind me.

"Excuse me. Are you Owen Keller?"

I spin around and am pleasantly shocked at who I'm looking at. "Hello again, Leopold."

"Tony. I didn't expect to see you," he says as he looks around nervously. "What is this place?"

"This is Fire and Ice."

He takes a few more cautious steps into the room. "Is this like a dance club or something?" he asks hesitantly.

"It's a BDSM club."

"Oh. I've heard of that before." He looks at me, his ocean-blue eyes widening, drawing me in deeper. "Do you work *here*, too?"

"If you're interested, we always have informational sessions," Owen interrupts us as he steps out of the kitchen and wipes his hands on a rag.

A tiny spark of hope ignites inside me. Maybe he'd be interested, but it's quickly extinguished when he ignores Owen's offer.

"I'm not here for... I'm Leopold," he stumbles over his words. "I have a delivery."

"My apologies," Owen chuckles. "It's a pleasure to meet you. I'm Owen. This is—"

"Tony," Leo interrupts, smiling when he meets my gaze.

"You two know each other already?" Owen asks, surprised.

"We met a few weeks ago," I reply without breaking eye contact. I'm content to drown in their depths.

"I deliver to his restaurant, too," Leo says quickly. "Nice place you have here."

Leo's made several deliveries to *Italiano Desiderio*. Since our first meeting, I've planned ahead for his arrival and always have espresso and a plate ready for him when he arrives. Witnessing the pleasure Leopold experiences from such a small act has become something I look forward to—crave more of.

I wish I knew he was coming here. I would've made sure to have something for him to eat.

"I see," Owen says, giving me a questioning glance. "If you want to bring the hand cart this way, we can unload it in the kitchen."

"Sure." Leo follows, pulling the squeaky cart behind him.

"I'll give you two a hand," I offer, knowing it'll give me a chance to see what Owen's been cooking. Hopefully, there's extra so I can to invite Leo to join us.

Owen's whipped-up chicken stir fry and noodles. Thankfully, there's enough for an army.

"Owen and I were just about to have a late lunch. Would you care to join us?" I ask as casually as possible.

"I don't want to intrude," Leo says, uncertainty clouding his features. And something else. Is it fear?

"I made plenty. You're more than welcome to stay." Owen pins me with a curious glance.

"Are you sure?" Leo bites his lip.

"Of course." This time, it's me who answers too quickly. I wasn't expecting to see Leo today. But now that he's here, I don't want him to leave.

He hesitates, and I think he'll say no until he asks, "Do you have a phone I can use to let Jerry know I'll be longer than expected?"

"There's a phone at the front desk," I say. My eyes track Leo as he walks across the room and out to the club's entrance, where the phone is located.

"You're awfully eager to not let him leave," Owen says quietly.

"Me?" I try to make light of my reaction, a light-hearted chuckle escaping me. "He's been delivering to my place, too. Leo's new to the city, and I get the feeling he doesn't have many friends here. He's always kinda down on himself," I explain. "I try to have something for him to eat and drink so he doesn't rush right out. Just trying to show him some kindness."

"Mhm." Owen clicks his tongue.

"The food looks ready." I attempt to divert his attention away from me. "I'll make our plates while you put that stuff away."

Leaving the dishes under the warmer, I bring out the cutlery. Leo doesn't hear me, so I have the chance to watch him. He walks past the stages, pausing to look at each one. For a moment, I allow myself to imagine Leo on one of them while I drizzle hot wax over his naked body.

I shake my head, knowing that train of thought is a slippery slope, and bring the silverware to the table. When I look up again, Leo's attention is fixed on Kameron's memorial. I walk over and stand near him.

"I'm so sorry," Leo says quietly.

"Kam was a good man," I murmur, my gaze fixed on the picture of him and me side by side.

"You two looked very happy together."

"We were."

"So, I guess you don't just work here." Leo turns his attention to me. "You're a part of all this."

"I am," I say and nod slightly. Something about this younger man makes me feel alive inside, and it's on the tip of my tongue to ask if it's something he's into as well.

"Soda or sparkling water," Owen interrupts as he calls from the kitchen doorway."

"Water," Leo and I answer in unison.

The moment slipping away, I say, "Come on and have a seat. I'm going to help Owen get the food."

Taking our seats at the table, the three of us start to eat. I pay close attention as Leo takes his first bite. He consistently savors whatever food is on his plate, and I take pleasure in watching his reactions.

"Are you a chef too?" he asks Owen.

"No," he chuckles. "I just enjoy getting in the kitchen every now and then."

"Well, this is delicious," Leo says as he savors another bite. "Thank you again for inviting me."

"Tony told me you're new to Manhattan. Where are you from?"

"California."

"Whereabouts? I have family in San Jose."

"I'm originally from Rolling Hills," Leo says between bites.

"What brings you all the way out here?"

I don't miss the almost imperceptible way Leo tenses before he mumbles, "I was looking for a change of scenery, I guess." And just like every time I ask too many questions about him, Leo changes the subject. "You said you aren't a chef, but I assume you work here."

"I'm co-owner of Fire and Ice."

"Oh," Leo says, surprised. "Does everyone in this city own their own business?"

Owen laughs. "Not the question I was anticipating."

A blush creeps up Leo's cheeks. There's something about his innocence that's arousing.

"I wasn't sure what's proper to ask." He shrugs.

"This is a safe space to ask any questions you have," Owen says, his tone serious.

Sex clubs of any kind are still viewed as taboo by much of society. Leo's reaction is not uncommon for us to hear. It's the hope of all of the more senior members of Fire and Ice to educate interested people and provide a safe environment to practice the BDSM lifestyle on a community level.

Leo looks at his watch, and not for the first time I realize I've never seen him with a cell phone. That's curious in a day and age when practically everyone has one. "Thanks, that's a very nice offer." He wipes his mouth and sets the napkin next to his plate. "But I have to get back to the store."

"Give me a minute," I say and get up quickly. "I'll get you something to bring the rest of your lunch with you."

"Thanks." Leo smiles.

Another thing I've noticed about Leo is how grateful he is when I package his leftovers. It makes me wonder about his situation, but I don't want to spook him with such personal questions. Grabbing a take-home container, I put the rest of the stir fry into it before returning to the table.

"Owen made enough for an army," I say. "I hope you don't mind that I put some extra in here."

"Not at all. I appreciate it very much, Tony," he says, gracing me with a smile that makes his eyes sparkle.

"I'll walk you to the door," Owen says. "I have a list of things we forgot to put on this week's order."

Leo gives me a small wave before following Owen out front. I'm envious. I wish it was me getting those extra few minutes with Leo.

Anthony

I'VE BEEN IN COURT EVERY DAY FOR THE PAST TWO weeks for Levi Young's trial. Although he's a minor, given his history and the fact he was involved in a hate crime, the state was able to try him as an adult. Thankfully, I wasn't called to testify. Levi didn't plead guilty, but the evidence against the seventeen-year-old was damning, allowing the state to wrap up their case reasonably quickly. His counsel did their best to mitigate the damage, but it didn't do much good. The jury only deliberated for two hours before returning with a guilty verdict on all counts.

Today is his sentencing. I've grappled with my emotions every day while sitting in the courtroom, watching this young man, his head hung low, as the evidence against him was presented. But it wasn't the crimes he was accused of that struck me most.

"Mr. Genovese," Judge O'Malley says my name, interrupting my internal thoughts. "I'm told you wish to address the court before Mr. Young's sentence is delivered."

"Yes, Your Honor." I get to my feet and am ushered to a podium with a microphone.

"Like yourself, Your Honor, I've been present in your courtroom each day listening to the case made against Mr. Young and the defense counsel's statements about his role in the crime. I don't possess your knowledge and understanding of the law," I say respectfully. "However, I do have the experience of being there during the crime itself."

I turn so I'm facing Levi, intending to address him directly. "We haven't been formally introduced. I'm Tony Genovese. You know now that the place of business you vandalized is my restaurant. I don't know how much your attorney has told you about me. I want to tell you a little bit, if it's okay with you, Your Honor?" I look to the judge, who nods.

"I'm a second-generation Italian-American. My grandparents married while young—Nonna was sixteen, and Nonoo was seventeen. With the dream of finding prosperity in the United States, they left everything behind. They immigrated from Sicily shortly after their marriage. They were proud of their Italian heritage, but in many ways, they were even prouder to call themselves Americans." I flip to my next page of notes.

"My parents fostered my love of cooking the meals I learned to prepare as a little boy with my Nonna. They also encouraged my dream of having my own restaurant—which should've been open a long time before that night, but September 11th happened."

"My partner, Kameron, was a fire chief in the FDNY. Kameron was one of the first rescue workers to respond after the first plane hit. While most people were running away, he looked fear in the face, and he ran toward the burning buildings. He was inside the North Tower when it collapsed. Kam didn't make it out." Levi's head pops up, and his wide eyes meet mine. "Opening that restaurant was a dream he and I shared together, but it was one I was forced to see come true alone."

"I've lost a lot of people in my thirty-eight years, but losing Kameron was the single most difficult thing I've ever endured. I learned what it's like to feel truly alone. The night you and your buddies paid my establishment a visit, I found myself at a crossroads. After hearing the hateful things you yelled about me—to me, I considered ending my life. I prayed for death." A hush descends upon the courtroom as I speak. "I ended up in the emergency room because they thought I had a heart attack. God, it hurt. It hurt so bad."

I take a second to compose myself before continuing, "Hate has always been part of the world, but on September 11th, hate took center stage. The men who hijacked those planes and altered the course of the entire world were pure evil. Being compared to the terrorists felt like the final blow for me." Images of the plane slamming into the side of the building sweep through my mind.

"There's been a lot of focus on the property damage incurred during your crime. But you know what? I don't care that the windows were smashed. That's fixable. Anyone who sees it now will never know they were at one time broken. But the words, the hateful words that were spoken. The names I was called—"

"Once upon a time, I was like this paper." I hold up a clean, white sheet. "As I've gone through life, especially after I came out as a gay man, I've been on the receiving end of ridicule and hate more times than I'd like to recall. My heart, like this paper, became damaged." I crumble it until it's in a ball. Then, I work to open it back up as I continue, "Each time I heal, but like this paper, I will never be unwrinkled. No matter how much you smooth it, there will always be wrinkles. You see, that's the problem with words and why they must be spoken with great care." Tears slide down Levi's cheeks. "Words can never be unspoken. No amount of punishment or apologies can erase the pain they inflict."

"Your right to have those thoughts and opinions isn't why you're on trial today. The founding principles of our country protect your right to voice your opinions. You could've made signs and even marched through this city blasting your beliefs, and no one would've been able to stop you. But I'd like to ask you to think about what I will say next. Our country is at war with the ideals of terrorism—one of the crimes you've been convicted of. Men and women, boys not much older than you are right now, are overseas, putting their lives in harm's way to protect each of us. To protect you and ensure you continue living in a country where you're free to voice your opinions," I pause.

"Depending on your sentence, you may go to jail, still being kept safe, while our soldiers fight on the front line. Many will lose their lives to ensure you continue to live in a land where you have a voice. How will you choose to use your voice moving forward?"

I flip to the last of my notes. "The crimes you've been convicted of are grave. Because this isn't your first offense, the state is asking for the maximum penalty. You're facing the potential of spending the next decade or so behind bars." Just saying that out loud makes my heart pound. "It's been suggested to me that I stand here and petition the court to impose the strictest punishment on you. I've been told that I should *want* to see you in prison. That you deserve it and the streets would be safer with you behind bars. I'm told that's how I'll get closure and heal from the trauma your actions inflicted on me," I say, taking a moment to let the gravity of my statement sink in. "But that's not what I'm here to do."

A murmur fills the courtroom.

Judge O'Malley bangs her gavel. "Order in the court," she calls. She waits until the people have settled before saying, "Please continue, Mr. Genovese."

"Your Honor, I'm asking you today to look at Levi Young, not the troubled young man convicted of these crimes, but try to see him like I've seen him. Levi is a seventeen-year-old boy—not much more than a child, yet somehow, he was involved in a very adult crime. How did that happen? Who was looking out for him? I've been in the courtroom every day for the past two weeks and noticed that with the exception of the free counsel he was afforded by the provisions of the law, no one has been here to support him." I glance at Levi, whose head is lowered as tears continue to fall. "I don't know his story. I don't know where his family is or why he doesn't have anyone supporting him and showing him unconditional love and support. I don't have to have those answers to know that sending an impressionable young man to prison when he's on the cusp of adulthood won't benefit him. It's not going to fix anything."

The judge studies me curiously before she speaks. "What are you suggesting?"

"In the days following September 11th, I spent countless hours volunteering to feed the rescue workers. I was able to witness firsthand how those efforts affected them. I also experienced healing within myself that I believe only comes through the giving of one's time." I turn so I can look at both Judge O'Malley and Levi. "Despite the nature of the crime and Mr. Young's participation in it, when I look at this young man, I don't see a hardened criminal the likes of which time in prison is the only answer. I do believe time in prison will only harden his heart and ensure when he's released, there will be no hope for him."

"The criminal justice system's goal is not only to punish criminals but also rehabilitate them and reintegrate them into society. I'm asking the court to forgo the maximum penalties and instead choose community service and education."

Once again, the courtroom erupts in shocked chatter. "Please continue," Judge O'Malley says after again silencing the audience.

"Our city is filled with opportunities for Mr. Young to give of his time to help others. To perhaps meet a caring adult willing to take him under their wing and to learn imperative life lessons that will serve him better than time spent in a jail cell. Levi," I say, waiting for him to lift his head. He watches me intently. "You've listened to everything I've said. You know how deeply wounded I was that night. I want you to know that I understand the anger and fear you felt after September 11th. It's an anger and fear I shared with you, but it's one we chose to express in very different ways. When you were questioned about that night, you asked for forgiveness. I want you to know—to hear from me, that I forgive you." My voice cracks with emotion.

"What happened is over. It's part of your past. Do not allow it to shadow your future." Levi blinks through his tears but doesn't break eye contact. "I don't know what's going to happen now—what sentence the court will impose. Whatever it is, whatever happens from here, I ask that you move forward and make a positive impact on the world. If each of us chooses to be the light, we'll extinguish the darkness, and the world will change. I believe in you."

I step away from the podium and return to my seat.

"I hope everyone in my courtroom never forgets what occurred here today. Mr. Genovese," the judge addresses me. "Every day, but especially in the wake of the tragedy that occurred on September 11th, the kindness you've just shown is an example of the kind of person we all should strive to be. You had every reason to hate, yet you chose compassion and forgiveness. I, for one, will never forget what I witnessed today." She clears her throat. "The court calls a one-hour recess, at which time we'll reconvene, and I'll hand out the sentencing."

"All rise," the bailiff calls out. Everyone gets to their feet and waits for the judge to exit before they file out of the courtroom.

"Thank you for everything," I shake the district attorney's hand.

"Do you want to grab a quick lunch before we return to hear the outcome?"

"No, thank you. I've said my peace. I won't be returning to see what the judge decides."

I walk out of the courtroom, filled with a sense of peace. I hope my actions have a positive impact, even in some small way. It's all a person can hope to do.

Leopold

I'VE LOOKED THROUGH MY ROOM AT LEAST TEN TIMES and can't find it. It's gone. The last of the money Donnie gave me, three hundred dollars—my rent money, is gone. One of my roommates must've been in my room, and there's nothing I can do about it. I can't prove that I had it or that it's gone. Again, my stupidity rears its ugly head.

What am I going to do now? The rent is five hundred dollars, and I only have two hundred in my bank account. I haven't squandered anything, either. After taxes and all the other deductions, my paycheck is only a little over six hundred dollars. I bought groceries and paid my share of the utilities two weeks ago. The cash I had here, along with the money I saved from last week's paycheck, would've covered it. I was going to stop by their office on the way to work.

Now, what am I going to do? I pace back and forth, trying to come up with a plan.

Phil and Maureen, the couple who run the program, always tell us to call if we need anything. I've never taken them up on their offer, but I have no other options. I'm glad the other guys are all at work right now because I don't want them eavesdropping on my conversation.

I make my way to the kitchen, where the house phone is located. We're required to have a landline. My roommates think it's old-fashioned to have one. That's easy for them to say. They all have cell phones. It's essential for me because I don't have one.

"Hello?"

"May I speak to Phil?"

"Speaking."

"Hi. It's Leo Wagner." I try to keep my voice calm and even.

"Hello, Leo. How are you?"

"I'm doing okay."

"What can I do for you?" Phil asks.

"I'm a bit short on my rent money," I say. "I was wondering if I could pay you what I have today and get you the rest after I get paid."

"When do you get paid?"

"Next Friday?" My words come out more like a question than a statement.

"Unfortunately, that's not going to work. The program agreement only allows a forty-eight-hour grace period."

"I've never been short or late. I have two hundred today. I promise I'll get you the rest the minute I get paid," I beg.

"There's no exceptions to our policy," Phil says. "If we let you do that, we'd have to let everyone, and that won't work."

I thread my fingers through my hair and grab it tight. "What can I do?"

"You can try borrowing money from a friend."

"Yeah, maybe." I can't tell him I have no friends here. "If I can't get the funds. What happens?"

"Like I said, you have a forty-eight-hour grace period. If at the end of that you don't have it, you'll be asked to leave the program and the apartment immediately."

"Where will I go?"

"That's up to you." There's a pause. "Why don't you come and drop off what you have. Maybe you can ask your boss to give you an advance for the rest?"

I don't want to have to ask Jerry for a loan, but there's not much else I can do. But at least it'll buy me a little time. "I'll be there shortly."

When I walk into the shop, I look around but don't see Jerry in any of his typical spots.

"Zeke, have you seen Jerry?" I ask my co-worker.

He doesn't look up from whatever he's doing on his cell phone when he mumbles, "He's in the hospital."

"The hospital?" My anxiety level spikes. "What's wrong?"

"How should I know? Someone's in his office. Go ask them."

I hurry down the back hall and find the door open. A woman is sitting at his desk, her back is to me. "Excuse me," I say without entering.

She spins the chair. "Hi."

"Zeke told me Jerry's in the hospital. What happened? Is he okay?"

"And you are?" she asks.

"I'm Leo. I work here. Is Jerry okay?" I ask, my words hurried.

"I've heard Uncle Jerry talk about you," she says. "We're not ready to discuss what's happening with his employees."

"Oh."

She grabs a stack of papers off the desk. "What time are you scheduled to work until? I can't find anything in this mess of papers." She makes a big deal of flipping through the ones in her hand. "I've told him he needed to switch to a computer system for years. This is a mess," she mutters.

"I work until close," I say. "I usually do the deliveries first and then return and take care of the stock."

"We already sent someone out with today's deliveries. Here it is." She pulls out a paper with the handwritten schedule. "We didn't get any new stock today. Do you know how to run the register?"

"No." Jerry never trained me on any of that. "I do all the back-room stuff."

"It's your lucky day then."

"What do you mean?"

She looks up at me. "There's nothing for you to do, so you get some extra time off."

"No new stock doesn't mean there's no work. The stock room still needs to be swept. I have to tally the—"

The woman holds up her hand. "I'm not worried about any of that right now. You're free to go." She spins her chair back to the desk, dismissing me.

Quietly, I walk a few aisles over to avoid Zeke. I don't feel like talking to anyone. Jerry's more than my boss. He's also my friend. And I have no idea what's happening with him. Selfishly, I didn't get a chance to ask about an advance on my paycheck, and even worse, they sent me home, so I'm not earning anything tonight.

This cannot be happening. "What the hell am I going to do?"

Leopold

It's Christmastime in the city. Everyone says it is the most wonderful time of the year. I question their logic. This is my second year here, and I'm still shocked by the sheer number of people descending upon this island for the Christmas shopping season. Busy and congested are understatements.

Last Christmas, Ramiro and his family flew out to spend the holiday with me. I stayed at the Plaza Hotel with them, where they ensured I had the whole holiday experience. Unfortunately, they can't make it this year. Ramiro and his wife, Jacinta, are expecting their third baby any day, so they aren't able to travel.

Every day, I watch couples walking hand-in-hand, their love for one another evident. Families smile and laugh as they take selfies in front of the many iconic decorations throughout the city. Everyone seems to have someone except me. I'm alone, and unless I get a miracle, I'm about to become homeless.

I've just gotten out of the shower and am getting dressed when there's a knock on the bathroom door.

"There's a phone call for you," my roommate calls through the door.

"Okay. I'll be right out." It has to be Ramiro. I've been waiting for his call to tell me the baby's here. I didn't want it to come to this. To tell him I screwed up and that I needed his help, but I'm desperate. It's the middle of the winter, and I'm facing being homeless. It's humiliating, but I'll work hard at repaying him. Someone in this city has to be willing to hire me. Even without a GED, I'll find a second job.

Quickly, so I don't keep him waiting, I pull on my jeans and throw my sweatshirt over my head. With my socks in hand, I hurry to the shared kitchen where the phone is. "Congratulations."

"What? Uh. Leo?"

"Who's this?"

"It's Billy. From work."

"Hi," I say hesitantly. "What's up?"

"I know you're scheduled to come in today, but... I don't know how to say this, man." My stomach sinks. "Jerry's dead."

I grab the counter for support. "Dead?"

"You know they brought him to the emergency room yesterday," he says. "I guess he had a stroke or something and never woke back up." I can't believe what I'm hearing. "You still there, Leo?"

"Yeah. I'm here. Are you at the store?"

"Not anymore. I got there this morning to start my shift, and his niece was there again," he explains. "She was putting a sign on the door that the store is closed indefinitely."

"Closed?" I ask, my voice barely above a whisper.

"She said when they figure out his estate, they'll be in touch to get us our final paychecks." This can't be happening. I pinch myself, half-expecting to wake up from a cruel dream. "I figured I'd save you a trip."

"Thanks," I mumble.

"No problem. Merry Christmas."

I can't answer him. I'm left speechless, the weight of the moment silencing me, and I hang up without saying goodbye.

The news of Jerry's passing has cast a heavy shadow over my world. In the wake of this loss, I find myself not only unemployed but also on the brink of homelessness. The ground I stood on has collapsed, and once again, I face an uncertain future.

Sensing the walls closing in, I have to escape before I suffocate.

Quickly grabbing my coat, I hurry out the front door.

I've been walking the streets of New York City for hours, attempting to wrap my head around everything that's happened today. But try as hard as I might, none of it makes sense.

My stomach growls, and I realize I haven't eaten all day. I reach into my back pocket for my wallet, but it's empty.

"Shit." In my hurry to leave the house, I must've forgotten to grab it. I have no choice but to walk back across town to get it.

I'm not even halfway there when the sky unleashes a torrent of ice-cold rain. I arrive back at the building thoroughly soaked and shivering. I enter my code, but the lock doesn't open.

I must have pressed the wrong button. Removing my bulky gloves, I give it another try, but the lock remains unresponsive. Growing frustrated and sensing an issue with the lock system, I press the buzzer. I wait anxiously, but no one answers. I try my code several more times. That's when the harsh reality slams into my chest.

I yank the elastic of my coat sleeve over my wrist to check my watch. It's seven pm. "No. No. No." The deadline for delivering the rest of my rent to Phil was five pm. After Billy's call, I lost all train of thought. In my hurry to get away, I completely forgot about calling Ramiro.

Sitting on the wet concrete stoop, I drop my head into my hands. How did everything fall apart so fast?

Ignoring the doorbell is a common occurrence with my roommates. I resign myself to waiting out here and catching them before they go out tonight. Hopefully, they don't act like their typical asshole selves and take pity on me just one time. Then, they never have to see me again.

The hours pass. The rain turns into snow. I'm soaked and freezing. Before I know it, it's midnight. The guys must've left early. Once they're gone, they won't be back until Sunday evening.

What am I going to do now? Where do I go?

Once again, I find myself wandering with no destination in mind. I don't realize where I'm at until I stop outside of the market. Is it too much to hope that Billy was playing a horrible joke on me? Yet, even from a distance, I notice the bright yellow paper taped to the door. As I approach, I read the handwritten note, "Closed Indefinitely."

This isn't a nightmare, and I'm not waking up from it.

"There's no loitering," a security guard calls.

"Sorry. I'm leaving."

I walk the few blocks to Hudson River Park. In the daylight, it's a bustling spot for locals and tourists to stroll along the river's edge. However, at nearly midnight, there's no one around. I stand by the metal rail, gazing out into the darkness. My heavy breaths are visible in the cold air.

I thought I was doing good this time. I meticulously followed every rule, crossing every T and dotting every I. I had a steady job that I loved and was studying for my GED and learner's permit. Jerry told me once I had my driver's license and could drive the delivery truck, I'd be getting a raise.

Jerry.

The pain cuts like a knife.

Jerry's dead. Just like that, I lost a father figure. The only person in this city who cared about me. I've held back tears all day, but now, in the darkness, I allow them to spill over and slide down my cheeks.

In a matter of hours, my life has fallen apart. I have nothing.

My hands are freezing, I stick them in my pockets, but they're not there. Instead, my hand touches something cold and hard. My boxcutter.

It's a sign. A small voice in my head whispers. *You're a screw-up. You have been since you were sixteen.*

"That's not true," I whisper into the night air.

Nothing's ever going to change. The voice grows louder. *You're just not good enough.*

Pushing the shiny silver blade out, I acknowledge that maybe that voice is right.

Just do it. No one's going to miss a worthless loser like you. Get it over with.

I *am* worthless, just like my father and David always told me. I've tried my hardest to make something of myself. To prove they were wrong, and look where it's gotten me. Nowhere.

I no longer feel the cold or the pain. The noise and lights of the city behind me fade as I push the blade against my wrist.

Epilogue

ANTHONY

The club is still packed with people for our annual Christmas Eve Eve party. I must be getting old. It's not even midnight, and I'm ready to leave.

"I'm going to head out," I say to Owen, who's talking with a small group of people.

"Already?"

"I had a long day at the restaurant. I'm beat."

"No problem." He smiles. "What time's dinner?"

For as long as I can recall, my house has been the gathering place for all my friends without family on Christmas dinner. It's become a tradition we look forward to. "Six, but I'll be there all day. You're welcome to come over whenever."

"Okay. I'll text you tomorrow."

Several people stop me on my way out to exchange Christmas greetings. I stop for only as long as is necessary to be polite before excusing myself. Then, I continue toward the door.

The rain has finally switched to lightly falling snow. It's the perfect backdrop for the holiday. I'd intended to go directly home, but a stirring in my soul urges me to walk along the pier.

Kameron and I used to love walking this path, but I've avoided the area since he died. I try to again tonight, not wanting to face those painful memories, but an irresistible force compels me.

A serene tranquility envelopes the area. The only sound is the gentle water lapping against the concrete wall.

A flicker of movement up ahead captures my attention. With each step forward, the silhouette by the river's edge slowly becomes clearer.

"Leopold?"

When I say his name, he startles and spins around. As he does, something falls from his hand and bounces off the metal lamp post with a ping before landing on the concrete.

It's a razor.

"Tony?" he asks, his voice trembling.

"What are you doing out here?"

"I was... Um..." He brushes his face, leaving a streak of blood on his cheek.

A razor.

Blood.

My body tenses with the realization of what he was about to do.

"I don't have anywhere to go," he confesses, his voice choked up with tears.

"Tell me what's going on," I say softly.

"Where do I start?"

"Wherever you're comfortable." I approach him cautiously, taking a tentative step to avoid startling him. "I want to understand."

"My roommates stole my money, leaving me short on cash. While I was trying to figure that out, I got a call that Jerry died, and I no longer have a job." He runs his hands through his hair. "I'm a hot mess. A loser with nowhere to go and no one who gives a shit if I live or die."

I open my arms, and he collapses into them, his body trembling as he cries.

The realization of why I had to come this way is clear. I'm certain Kameron had something to do with this. Silent tears escape from my eyes as I hold Leo in my protective embrace.

"I'd care," I whisper.

Loving each other changed Anthony and Leopold forever.

Now they're left facing the hardest question of all, what happens when love alone no longer feels like enough?

Because even the strongest hearts can break before they finally heal.

Continue the Fire & Ice series finale in *Love Heals*.

Find Tara's Books Here

About Tara

Bestselling author Tara Conrad writes where passion meets peril, crafting dark, spellbinding romances that blur the line between devotion and destruction.

Inspired by the haunting brilliance of Edgar Allan Poe, her stories reimagine Gothic tales with modern sensuality and power.

Within her pages, heroines rise unbroken, villains fall beautifully, and the darkness always tells the truth.

When she isn't writing, Tara travels with her husband, meeting readers who have found pieces of themselves in her worlds.

She believes love isn't always light. Sometimes, it's found in the dark. 🖤

Acknowledgments

First and foremost, I want to thank my husband. George- You're the reason I'm able to write these books. I know you don't think so, but without your help, none of this would happen. You're always there to talk me off the ledge when I'm stuck. When the storyline is getting dull, you throw in a plot twist for me. When I write the same word 845723L5 in one paragraph, you help me clean it up. Let's not forget all the readthroughs you listen to. There's no one else I'd want to do this with. I love You, Sir

George, Jacob, and Kayla- You're the three still living at home. Thank you for helping pick up the slack while I'm deep in my writing cave, trying not to miss the next deadline. George and Jacob-thank you for selling my books to your co-workers and anyone else you talk to. Kayla, thank you for your editing help, proofing all my audiobooks, and being one of my best friends.

Rebekah, Jonathan, and Baby E- It goes without saying to thank you for the gift of Baby E. He's been such a light in our lives this past year. Baby E- thank you for being Nana's best PA ever. You make writing very exciting. Especially when you rearrange my whole manuscript. You're my favorite! Rebekah- Thank you for your creative in helping with my social media. I love our middle-of-the-night conversations and that you always have faith in me. Jonathan- thank you for your quiet support and for going through all the trouble of getting a new work schedule just so you can come to all my signings. ;-)

My Beta Team: Dana, Evonna, Kayla, Rebekah, and Sarah- All of you ladies are invaluable to me. I hope each of you knows how much I appreciate you and the care you take reading my books. I'm so thankful we were put in each other's lives. Here's to many more books in our future!

To each of my readers- thank you doesn't seem enough to convey my gratitude to everyone. Knowing you're reading my books and loving my characters as much as I do is amazing. I love each and every one of you and hope I get to meet you all one day soon.

~Tara

National Human Trafficking Resource Center 1-888-373-7888
TTY 711
Text HELP to 233733

ONLINE RESOURCES

www.dhs.gov/bluecampaign

polarisproject.org

humantraffickinghotline.org